CHOICES

A Love's Valley

Historical Romance

To the
Davis Library

CHOICES
•
Carolyn Brown

All my Best!

Carolyn Brown

PRINTED IN THE UNITED STATES OF AMERICA
ON ACID-FREE PAPER
BY HADDON CRAFTSMEN, BLOOMSBURG, PENNSYLVANIA

To my brother,
Douglas V. Gray,
With much love

Chapter One

Raymond Pierce was a worthless, rotten-to-the-core, gutter rat. The stage coach bounced along, hitting every rut, Texas dust finding its way through the curtain in the window where he sat all smug in a cloak of self-induced snobbish power. Douglass Esmerelda Sullivan hoped the dust choked him to death. If he keeled over at her feet, with a parched, grime-coated throat, dying of thirst, she wouldn't even uncap the canteen of water beside her. He'd deceived her with his smooth talking lies and she'd believed him. Now she'd learned an almighty hard lesson the worst way possible. Her reputation was ruined. Her father would be scandalized; her mother, mortified. Her brothers? That six pack of pure Mexican-Irish anger would probably hunt Raymond down and send him to have an upclose and personal visit with St. Peter himself when they found out the way he'd duped her.

When they got finished with Raymond, it would be her turn to face their wrath, and what those brothers would do with her produced cold shivers up and down Douglass' spine in spite of the hot, Texas heat. Esmie loved the world she'd lived in. Loved her family. Adored all six of her older brothers. Thought she'd loved Raymond. What she didn't love was the idea of a convent for the rest of her life and that's where they'd put her after the stunt she'd just pulled. Just like Uncle Miguel had done with his daughter when she'd

1

run away ten years ago. Esmie had never forgotten the day her cousin came home in tears, reputation ruined. No, sir, she did not want to join her cousin in the convent.

But that's what lay in store for her, she was sure. Her brothers would already be on their way to bring her home. At least she hoped they wouldn't believe the note she'd left, prayed they knew Raymond for the skunk he was rather than the knight in shining armor she had thought he was. Being the baby and only girl in a family of seven children, she'd grown up protected and spoiled. After this stunt, she would still be spoiled, but probably from within the confines of the nearest convent, where she would be very well protected for the rest of her life.

"You had no intention of ever marrying me?" she asked Raymond one more time.

"No, I did not intend to and will not marry you, Esmie, darling. My blue-blooded eastern mother would drop dead if I brought someone in with Mexican or Irish blood and introduced her as my wife. However, Esmie, we are going to have a fine time from here to Philadelphia. And there will be no repeats of last night, or I'll beat you half to death. You won't throw another hissy fit, you better understand that right now. And if I have to pay for another broken vase I will take my razor strop to you. I mean it. If you play those games again, you will be sorry. When we get to Philadelphia, I shall either purchase you a ticket back to this god forsaken dust-ridden place or give you that sum of money which will keep you until you can find a job. That's as much as you'll ever get from me," Raymond sneered, his thin lips setting in a fine line below a pencil-thin, blond mustache.

"You said you loved me when you asked me to run away with you," Douglass reminded him.

"I lied." He chuckled.

She glared at him, much the same as she'd done the night before when he rented one room in the hotel and expected her to sleep in the same bed with him without the benefit of a marriage license. "You are a worthless rascal and I hope when my brothers kill you it's a long and painful death."

"You are a spit fire, who I'm sure will be a delight in bed after you get used to the idea," he replied, laughing. "You are not an Irish princess, Esmie. You are just a half-breed Mexican-Irish lass and no one cares where you are. Your brothers aren't coming after you, Esmie. They'll be glad to get rid of something as spoiled and sassy as you are. Besides, you left a note, remember? They think you are eloping. What they don't know can't hurt them. You can return to Texas in a few months and tell them you are a widow or any other plausible lie to get back into their good graces. Now sit back on the seat. We've got the whole day to ride and then tonight, my darlin', you will give me my money's worth of a good time or else I will make you pay. You have no other alternative. I own you."

"No man owns me." She folded her arms over her ample bosom, wanting to weep but refusing to give Raymond the satisfaction of knowing he'd been able to reduce her to tears. "And there's always an alternative, Robert."

"Oh, and what is it?" He raised a light-colored eyebrow over green eyes.

Last week that same expression had caused little goose bumps to speed up and down her backbone. Today, it irritated her so much, she wanted to reach across the coach and slap fire from his cheeks and thunder from his ears.

He leaned forward and whispered. "Tonight, I will sleep with you and you will deny me nothing."

She put the palm of her hand on his nose and pushed him backwards, then slid across the wooden seat to the other window. Yes, there was an alternative. It might reap nothing but worse rewards, but at least that snake-in-the-grass who'd led her down the daisy path wouldn't be having his way. She slipped a gloved hand out of the window and knocked hard on the side of the coach.

"What the—" Raymond sneered.

"The alternative," she said sweetly around a lump in her throat as the coach came to an abrupt halt.

"Yes, ma'am?" The driver opened the door. "Pretty sparse around here if you're needing a bush to hide behind."

"No, sir," she said, stepping out of the stage. "I want you to unload my trunk right here. This is as far as I intend to go."

"This is ridiculous." Raymond followed her out into the blistering morning heat, shouting and shaking his fist as his face grew redder and redder. He wiped his brow with a snowy white handkerchief. "You cannot stay on the side of the road."

"I can and I will. That's my alternative," she said, tilting her chin up high and looking down her thin, aristocratic nose at the man she'd trusted just last week. "Get my trunk off the back of this thing right now."

"But ma'am, you're on your honeymoon and all," the driver said, shifting his eyes from one to the other.

"No, I thought I was, but this man has no intentions of marrying me. So this is where I get off this stage. Now are either of you going to unstrap my trunk or am I going to have to do it myself?" she asked, keeping fear and anger both from her voice of cold steel.

"I won't touch your trunk." Raymond folded his arms over his chest.

"I'll do it, but there's Indians, and Yankees going home, and rattlesnakes, not to mention highway pirates," the driver warned. He set the trunk on the ground and dust bubbled up high enough to make her sneeze.

"You can't do this," Raymond said.

"I'm nineteen years old, and I'll be twenty on my birth-day in a couple of months." She eyed the man who'd even begun to look like a gutter rat to her. "That's old enough to do what I want. You'll just have to find a different doxy in every hotel between here and the East, Raymond. That is until my brothers find you. You better sleep with a pistol in your hand and knife under your pillow. And let me tell you, living in a convent with nuns the rest of my life won't be as bad as what you'd have me to do. At least I've got my dignity, even if it is in tatters right now. I've kept it through the war, through the worry of wondering if my brothers would die in the fighting. Through it all. You are just a maggot compared to all that. So good-bye, Raymond. Driver, you'd best get on down the road now if you are going to make your schedule."

"Yes, ma'am," the driver grinned. She'd do alright, that one would, he figured. Anyone with that much spunk could probably take on the critters, both two-legged, four-legged, and those that crawled upon their bellies. "You staying with her or going on?" he asked Raymond.

"I'm not staying in this place a minute longer than I have to." Raymond huffed and got back into the coach without even looking back.

Esmie opened her trunk, drew out a lace-edged parasol, the pistol her grandmother gave her for her sixteenth birthday, and a clean, lace-edged handkerchief. She shut the lid with a bang, sat down on the top of the trunk, snapped open the parasol over her head, and placed the loaded pistol in her lap.

She fumed even though she wanted to curl up in a ball and cry until her blue eyes swelled shut and her throat ached from it.

Before the war there'd been plenty of men vying for her hand. When she was sixteen and dancing every week at a party in DeKalb, Texas, life was good and men abundant. She just had to fall in love with one of them and her future would be carved into the green hills of the horse country. But none of them made her heart do those funny things she'd heard about, and until a man did that, she wasn't having one. Not then, anyway. Then the War Between the States came and most of the able-bodied men chose sides and went to fight. She'd have gone with her older brothers to fight for the Confederacy but they didn't let girls join the Army. Her grandmother, Abulita Montoya, said that Michael Sullivan marked her when he gave her a boy's name. Granny was the one who insisted she be called Esmie by the family, but, sitting on the trunk in the middle of the road, Esmie suddenly hated the name. The way Raymond had sneered when it came from his mouth made her feel nauseated. Esmie fanned herself with the hanky as she thought back on the day her brothers rode off to war. She was trying to take her mind off Raymond Pierce, but it didn't work.

The years had gone by slowly, but finally the war ended and her brothers had come home. Raymond arrived not far behind them; a newspaper writer from the east coast doing stories about the land wars and the unrest in Texas. He and her brother Nicolaus had struck up a friendship and Nick had invited Raymond to stay at the ranch. The rest was history. He'd flirted behind the six brothers' backs and finally convinced Douglass to go with him when he left. She still didn't have that wonderful feeling in her heart, but she was nineteen now, and figured all that swooning and love-stuff was probably just the fabric of a young girl's dreams. It had no place in her reality.

Rivulets of sweat ran down her neck and between her breasts. When September came, it was supposed to cool off. She shoved the hanky down the bodice of her dress and mopped up as much as she could, but even before she removed it, the sweat beads were forming again. She had thought the coach was hotter than the devil's pitchfork and nothing could be worse, but she had been wrong again. Just like she'd been about Raymond Pierce.

He'd sweet talked her; told her she was so beautiful with her long, black hair and crystal clear blue eyes. He had begged her to run away with him to Philadelphia when he left Texas. They'd have a good life back East in Philadelphia. He'd continue working for the newspaper his father owned and all the men would swoon when they saw her on his arm at the opera or in the finer restaurants. The war was over. Life could go on.

Now that she thought about it, she realized he'd never ever

said the word marriage one time. That was her own stupid mistake. He had told her he loved her and she assumed that meant marriage if they ran off together. How could she have been so naive?

"Because that's what I *wanted* to believe," she said with a snort. "Well, I won't be fooled again. For sure if Daddy sends me to a convent. Cousin Bertha can teach me to meditate and pray. Lord, I hate to think of my brothers. Patrick is going to preach at me until my ears hurt. And Colum's temper will set the whole state on fire," she whispered, trying to keep herself company in the sweltering heat.

Surely by nightfall another stage coach would come by. It didn't matter which way it was going. Back to DeKalb, Texas to her mother's tears and her father's sharp Irish temper, or ahead to the next town in Arkansas. If the latter were the case, she'd use the money in the bottom of her trunk to rent a reputable hotel room and send her family a telegram to come get her. All that would do would be to prolong the journey to the nearest convent, so she really wished for a stage going back to the Texas town where she'd grown up. She wondered how she'd look in a nun's habit and wrinkled her nose at the vision.

She wondered what the nuns would think of a woman with a man's name. But that's what she would be from then on. Douglass. Never Esmie again. Not from any member of her family or even from the nuns. Every time she heard the name she'd be reminded of the sneer on Raymond's face when he used that endearment so hatefully, making it sound like a dirty word.

"If my brothers decide not to kill him, I hope he finds a woman who walks on him like he is a doormat," she said, snapping the hanky out in the still air, hoping to dry it so she could wipe more sweat from under her nose and her neck. This was the time of the day when she should be shucking out of her clothing and lying still on her bed for a long siesta, not sitting all trussed up in a corset by the side of the road on the most sweltering day of September.

Douglass peeped around the edge of the parasol to see what time it was. High noon according to the placement of the sun. The cook at their ranch house would be ringing the triangle bell for her brothers to come for lunch. Her stomach growled, reminding her that it had been a long time since supper the night before. She'd been so angry at breakfast she refused to even touch the tray Raymond had set before her.

"And with good reason," she said with a nod of her head, agreeing with herself for not eating.

The tray had held pancakes dripping with butter and syrup, a steaming cup of black coffee just like she liked, and a tall glass of chilled milk. The sorry rascal had probably thought she'd change her mind if he brought her food. Well, she hadn't then, and she never would. Not even if he came back on a white horse right now and promised to marry her at the next town. Not after last night's humiliation and the way he'd acted so condescending toward her in the stage.

She'd expected her own room, at least until they were officially married. But after supper, he'd told the man at the desk in the inn that they were on their honeymoon and needed one room. She'd started to raise a fuss then, but he'd squeezed her arm so tightly that it bruised. When they got to the room, he'd roughly dragged her into his arms for a kiss. Only it wasn't a sweet kiss like she'd been used to having from him. It was demanding and humiliating at the same time.

"Play time is over. Let's get down to the real business," he'd growled.

She'd reached behind her to the dresser he'd shoved her back against, picked up a vase and broke it over his head. He merely laughed and told her to take off her clothing. He'd waited all day for what was his due and he was ready to go to bed.

"Gabriel will dance a jig with the devil himself before I go to bed with you without a marriage license, Raymond," she'd responded vehemently. "And if you touch me again I will scream."

She'd never been afraid of anything in her life; not snakes

or spiders. Only heights had come close to making her afraid, and she'd never admitted that to anyone. Not when she had six older brothers who were just waiting to pounce on a weakness to tease her about. But at that moment, with Raymond demanding things that, for her, were sinful without benefit of marriage, Douglas had been terrified. However, she'd have been boiled in oil before she let him know it.

"Who'll listen? I'll just tell them you are a reluctant bride," he'd said.

A cornered rat will turn and fight for its life, and Douglass did too. She didn't say a word to the repulsive man who'd been so attractive as they planned their elopement. She had simply opened the lid of the trunk the man had lugged up the stairs and into the room, and, as if she were taking out the sheer, cotton nightrail she'd planned to wear on her wedding night, brought out her pistol.

"Now, *you* will listen," she'd said, pointing the gun right at his sorry black heart. "I intend to sit in that rocking chair all night. If you so much as come near me, I will shoot you, Raymond. I'm not going to bed with you without a marriage license. Right now I'm pretty sure I don't even want to marry you. I'll think about it through the night. Now you do whatever you want to, but don't you so much as look cross-eyed at me."

"You wouldn't shoot me," he'd challenged.

"Oh, darlin', I would. I really would," she'd smiled sweetly. "And God wouldn't even lay the sin to my charge. He'd probably set a big old ruby in my crown just for doing it. To think after a war, I actually trusted a Yankee. Now leave me alone to decide whether I even want to marry you."

"I won't marry you," Raymond had said bluntly, falling back on the bed and staring at the ceiling for a few minutes before he began to snore.

By morning he was a little sweeter; she was a lot sourer. She might have married him just to save her family the embarrassment, but it was probably for the best that she didn't. They would have both been dead within the sight of six months. No, she'd just wait on the side of the road and a stage would come by sometime. If not today, then tomorrow morning. Surely, she wouldn't starve by then.

Chapter Two

Monroe Hamilton was bone tired. Years of fighting produced nothing but a war torn country that would take decades to mend. Nothing would ever be the same again. Not even his farm. The last letter he had from his mother told him the house was still standing. They lived far enough back in the valley that the war hadn't destroyed their house and farm like in other places. Take Gettysburg and Chambersburg for instance; they'd lost so much. There were good crops in the Hamilton's field, and enough help to bring it to fruition. The cattle had faired well and the horses—his precious horses—were alive. His father had made shrewd investments before he died, and Monroe's mother had kept things going very well. The Hamilton family was still wealthy, but the old ways were gone in the North as well as in the South, and as much as he'd loved his father, Monroe was glad he wasn't alive to see what was left when civil war split a country wide open at the seams.

His mother had said in her letter that men were straggling back home, one or two at a time. His sister Indigo, who'd still been in pigtails and short skirts when he'd mounted his horse and rode out of Love's Valley in a blaze of glory, was now eighteen. He'd seen her briefly, along with his mother, when the war ended, but then he was sent to Galveston to help in the reconstruction of Texas. To hold the fort for a year until his commission was finished. His brothers, Henry

11

Reuben and Harry Reed, both younger than Monroe, would be coming home within the next year when their jobs were finished. He'd be glad to see them; glad to have their help on the acreage. His mother had also written that his cousin Ellie had come to live with them permanently when her parents were both killed in the fire at Chambersburg. Two young girls and his mother, holding down a whole valley, waiting patiently for the Hamilton men to return.

Monroe slipped a canteen from the saddlebags of his horse and drew deeply, tilting his head back and letting some water dribble down his shirt collar. He would have been farther along on the long trip home if he hadn't promised Thad Miller that he'd go by that little town south of Texarkana, Texas on his way home and give his father all the news from Galveston. Now Monroe had a long hard journey before him before he'd be back in the hills of Love's Valley, Pennsylvania. He had already vowed that if God would bring him home in one piece, he would never leave again. When Monroe made a vow, he stuck by it.

He'd deliver the messages the general sent along with him to six cities and pick up packages of reports to take to Washington D.C. on his way home, and then he'd consider his job completed. He planned to settle down on his farm and watch his brothers and sister, along with his cousin Ellie raise *their* families. Monroe knew he would never fall in love. It wasn't even an option. He wasn't the same twenty-three-year-old romantic soul who left Pennsylvania all those years ago. He'd been to a circus called war; he'd seen the big elephant called life. He'd seen men die for the cause on both sides of the Mason-Dixon line. He'd seen even more die from disease and hunger. No, it took a tender heart to fall in love, and Monroe's had been hardened with disgust.

He tried to shake off the gloom and despair by thinking about Ellie and Indigo. He'd see them before long, and the hard work he would be doing on the farm would keep him busy until Henry Reuben and Harry Reed came home. What he'd give to gather all of them into his arms in a family hug couldn't be measured by anything this side of paradise itself.

Monroe's eyes, so dark they looked black, looked ahead toward nothing but solitary riding; a long, lonely ride over more than a thousand miles with no one but himself, a horse, and a mule to visit with. Monroe pushed his collar-length black hair out of his eyes and readjusted his hat. By the time he'd been home a week, he'd be longing for a little solitude, what with all those women chattering all the time, he reminded himself as he rode along in quietness. Did they still fuss about whether someone would have on a dress just like theirs at a fancy ball? No, he didn't suppose they would. Mother had said they'd been troopers helping on the farm. She'd even mentioned that Indigo was quite a cook these days and that Ellie helped keep the stables. He shook his head just thinking of that sight; Ellie, with her long blond hair and pale eyes, mucking out a horse stall. It saddened him even more.

"Lord, here they come." Douglass shaded her eyes and looked at the dust cloud the horses kicked up. "Thirty-six hours and my life is ruined. They won't even have ridden off their anger by now." Well, she hadn't let Raymond see her weep, and she wasn't going to cry in front of her brothers either. She set her face in firm stone and prepared herself for the confrontation.

Should she faint and pretend to have heat stroke? It would be so easy. Just wait until they were nearly to where she still sat on the trunk, then simply fall off the side. When they revived her, she could pretend that her mind was addled and she couldn't remember a thing for the past two days. No, that wouldn't work. They would have gotten the note. Colum would shake her until her teeth rattled and her memory suddenly popped right back into her head.

The only thing she could do was look all six of them in the eye, tell them the truth, and then beg to ride with them to the next town where they'd find that scoundrel sleeping in his bed. She'd even offer to fire the first bullet into his black heart, but Nick could be sure he was going to shoulder part of the blame for this whole fiasco. He shouldn't have befriended a rascal like Raymond and brought him to the ranch. Yes sir, brother Nicolaus Fresco Sullivan could wipe that scowl off his face and accept the fact that if he wasn't so quick to make friends, she wouldn't be in this mess to begin with.

There were two horses but appeared to be only one rider; Douglass observed as she continued to stare into the western sun. Was she only worth one measly brother coming to rescue her? Her heart twisted up in a knot and rage burned from her light blue eyes. Which one was it? Probably Patrick, since he was the oldest. *Holy Mother of Jesus,* she earnestly prayed, *don't let it be Patrick. Let it be Flannon or even Nicolaus but not Patrick. He'll lecture me all the way back to DeKalb.*

Monroe saw something strange in the distance. It appeared to be a rock, but with a splash of bright pink right in the middle. He checked the position of the sun. No, it couldn't be a reflection from a small puddle of water. It *was* a rock and there was color on it. Now wasn't that the strangest thing he'd ever encountered. He rode slowly and kept his eyes on it, but it didn't move. The closer he got the more distinct the form became, until he determined it wasn't a rock but something square with a woman sitting on it.

He spurred his horse and rode faster. "What would a woman be doing sitting on the side of the road?" he wondered aloud. "And a lady at that, from the looks of that fancy parasol," he mumbled under his breath when he was only a hundred feet from her.

"Evenin', ma'am," he said. "You got troubles?"

Well, it sure wasn't one of the Sullivan boys, Douglass realized when she looked up into the blackest eyes of the handsomest man she'd ever seen. He looked harmless enough, but one could never be too sure. Raymond had been as loving as a new kitten and look what kind of mess that had turned out to be. Douglass knew she had to be on guard.

One minute Monroe was tipping his hat with a polite nod, the next he was looking down the double barrels of a lady's hand gun. He didn't reckon that those little bullets would kill him, but they could sure put out an eye or make a hole in his skin where infection could set up. He'd managed to fight the whole war without even a scratch, if you didn't count that time the *bois d'arc* branch hit him across the neck, and now some piece of fluff in petticoats was about to shoot him.

"You got a mind to steal my horse, lady?" he asked.

"I got a mind to sit right here and wait for the next stage. I'm just making sure you know that and that you ride right on past here," Douglass replied.

"But ma'am, there won't be a stage coming this way for a couple of days."

"You don't know that." She kept the gun trained on his handsome face.

"Oh, but I do. I thought about riding it for a while. At least from Texarkana, but after I found out I'd have to sit still a couple of days waiting for another one, I figured I could make better time on my own. Then I stopped in a little town this morning. They said the next coach would be coming through in two days. I kept riding," he said. "Now put away that gun and let's talk. Why are you sitting here in the broiling sun?"

"Waiting," she responded honestly. "You go on and leave me alone."

"No, I don't think so," Monroe said, that familiar feeling in his gut telling him that he should do what she said and not even look back. The feeling had never betrayed him before. Not in the war years. Not in the year since then. The war might have made beggers of the north and south both, but it didn't make rascals of all its men. He swallowed hard and ignored the feeling.

"Oh, yes you will," she said emphatically.

"I have a pack mule, carrying a small load of my supplies. I cannot leave a lady beside the road. You aren't very big, so you can ride the pack mule. There's one empty saddle bag. You'll have to leave that trunk, but you can take anything you can get in the saddle bag," he said softly. "I have a sister and a cousin at my place in Pennsylvania. I would hope no gentleman would leave any of them alone along the side of the road."

"Oh, my Lord, you are a Yankee," she groaned.

"I am that without a doubt."

"But you do look normal." She eyed him carefully.

"I assure you there are no horns under my hat," he told her, a tight little smile escaping from the corners of his mouth.

"Who are you?" she asked.

"Captain Monroe Hamilton of the Union Army. I'm going home. My enlistment is up. And you are at least going to the next town with me. I'd planned to ride through the backcountry to avoid highway pirates, but we can ride on to Arkadelphia, Arkansas. You should be safe there until a stage comes through. I cannot leave you in the middle of the road."

Gears began to turn in her mind. "Did you say Pennsylvania? How far is your home from Philadelphia?"

"Couple to three days by stage," he answered. "Just which way were you going?"

"I was going east. To Philadelphia," she said. That much wasn't a lie at least. She had been going to Philadelphia, supposedly as a new bride. "I have an aunt there who, bless her heart, married a Yankee. I was going to visit her." Now that *was* a lie, and the nuns would make her stay on her knees until she had calluses for telling it.

"Alone?" Monroe looked closely at the gun, still trained on his chest.

Douglass considered the situation. It was a long way to

Philadelphia, and several weeks would give her brothers plenty of time to cool their heels. They might actually be glad to see her if they'd been riding all that time. In that length of time they might forget their anger. Maybe they'd even spoil her on the trip back to Texas, they'd be so happy that she was alive.

Maybe they aren't even coming to get you. Doubt filled her head when she thought of what Raymond had said. If they weren't, then she was going to Philadelphia anyway. If she went home right now, she'd be in the same place Cousin Bertha was ten years ago. The choice was hers and she'd just made up her mind. Raymond Pierce was going to pay for his smart mouth, and Douglass was going to make him pay.

"Yes, alone. I made a grave error in judgment," she said, lowering the gun. "My reputation is ruined. A man I trusted said he would escort me all the way to Philadelphia then left me sitting right here because I wouldn't . . ." She blushed, her light brown skin turning scarlet.

"You wouldn't what?" Monroe asked, the prickly sensation on his neck getting even worse.

"I wouldn't go to bed with him without the benefit of a marriage," she said, looking him straight in the eye without so much as a blink. "I can't go back anyway. I'm an orphan." She checked the cloudless, blue sky for sudden lightning bolts. When they gave her a nun's habit, she'd swear then she'd never lie again. Until then, she'd just have to make do with whatever came to mind.

"You have no family and the escort treated you shamelessly. I will at least escort you to the next town," Monroe insisted. "Get what you want from that trunk. You wouldn't have any pants in there would you? My mule doesn't have a saddle, much less a lady's saddle, so you will have to ride astride."

"No, I don't have pants," she replied with indignation.

In five minutes, she'd crammed her little reticule with what cash she had, then stuffed his spare saddle bag with a change of underthings, the handmade lace *mantilla* and *peineta* her grandmother gave her on her sixteenth birthday, her gun, and a silver comb and brush set. When the Sullivan brothers came and found the trunk, they'd recognize the rest of her things and follow the trail. She purposely left her favorite shawl thrown on the ground.

She jerked her skirt tails up, ignored the flash of petticoats and lace-trimmed drawers, and slung a leg over the mule. She wasn't going to the next town to wait, no matter what Monroe Hamilton said. She was going to put at least two weeks, and maybe a month or more, between her and the Sullivan brothers. They'd come, she reassured her heart. She knew they would. They knew Raymond better than she did. She hung on to that hope at the mule began to follow Monroe Hamilton on his big, beautiful horse. She truly wanted to see them, but not right now. Not until they'd had time to get rid of the anger they had good reason to harbor towards her.

"What's your name?" Monroe asked, trying to ignore the empty sensation in his stomach. It was hard to explain, but it never, ever failed him. Once that sensation started, there was trouble on the wind. Evidently, this trouble came in the form of a lovely young lady. The least he could do was find out her name.

"My name is Douglass," she said, riding the mule like she'd been born on a horse.

"Oh, sure it is." He threw back his head and laughed. "That's a man's name. Or is it your last name?"

"It's my first name. My momma's Mexican and my father Irish. They made a deal. Poppa could give all the kids their first names and Momma would provide the second name. After six sons, Poppa didn't think there was a possibility of a daughter so he chose the name Douglass. When I turned out to be a girl he was speechless, so the name stayed the same."

"And where pray tell do all six of these brothers live? You said you are an orphan," he asked, raising an eyebrow.

"They're scattered. The war, you know," Douglass replied evasively. She'd been caught in her first lie. She'd have to be more careful about her stories for sure.

"And what is your middle name?" he asked.

"That is none of *your* business," she said. "What is your middle name?"

"My name is Monroe Hamilton," he answered quickly.

"That's two last names. What goes in the middle?" she asked.

"My middle name is Monroe and my first name is none of *your* business," he said testily. "We will have to make a camp tonight because the next town is too far away to reach. But tomorrow you can send a telegram to your brother. I bet you know where one of them is, anyway. And he can come and get you. You will go back, face the music, and get it over with," he continued, both changing the subject and making sure she knew that this was only a twenty-four hour deal. No more, and hopefully a lot less. Monroe wasn't the tracker his brother Henry Reed was, but he could smell a lie a mile away. Douglass didn't want to go home because her reputation was ruined. She most assuredly was not an orphan or he'd fry his spurs and have them for breakfast. The family had trusted the wrong escort to take her to Philadelphia, and she'd be the one who paid the piper for that misplaced trust.

Chapter Three

As the sun dropped behind the trees on the horizon Monroe shot a rabbit. With that and a pan of hoe cake, they could have supper. Douglass had begun to look faint a while back, but she'd never said a word. She simply sat on the mule riding far enough behind him to prohibit conversation, which was fine with Monroe. If he didn't know the girl, then it wouldn't be any big deal to leave her waiting in a hotel for her brothers. He tried to imagine what he'd do if Indigo had pulled some kind of hare-brained stunt like that. First he'd make the man who deceived her wish for death, then he'd take his sister home and call the nuns at the nearest priory to come and get her. It would be the only option left for him. Her reputation would be in shambles and no decent man would ever want to marry her. Everyone in the area would look down on her so the priory would be the only place for her to maintain at least some form of dignity.

For some reason, the spunk Douglass had shown in getting out of the stage and putting herself on the road reminded him of his sister. Indigo might have made an impulsive decision and ruined her reputation, but she wouldn't let any man take advantage of her.

Reflecting on the palpable silence, Douglass wondered if Captain Monroe Hamilton was always so quiet or if he just didn't like the added burden of having a woman along on the trip. Well, he wouldn't have to put up with her for very long. She had formed a plan as they rode east, the sun setting behind them in a blaze of colors. Stealing his horse and riding away in the dark would be simple enough. She had enough money to keep her for at least a month. He'd mentioned Arkadelphia, Arkansas; that's exactly where she wouldn't go. She'd ride west for at least a day, then she'd cut back south and then west again. By then Monroe would be long gone on his way back to his home in some valley he'd mentioned.

She was so tired and so tied up in her own thoughts, Douglass had practically jumped off the mule when Monroe drew his gun and fired at the rabbit. When her wits settled, her mouth watered at the thought of fried rabbit. She'd eat well; it might be a while before she found a town with a hotel where she could hide out and find her next meal. Surely they didn't hang women who stole horses. Of course not, especially if they never found her or the horse. Besides, she'd see to it that her brothers made it right with the good Captain Hamilton after they found her. She'd tell them how chivalrous he was and how he'd loaned her the horse to come back home, but she'd gotten lost.

Lies, her conscience scolded her with one word.

"Hush," she mumbled under her breath. "A few lies may be necessary to keep me out of a nun's habit. Oh why did I listen to that Raymond Pierce? And why did Nick bring him home?"

"Talking to me or to yourself?" Monroe asked when he found what he deemed the perfect camp site in a hollow surrounded by trees.

"Myself," she answered, sliding gracefully from the mule's back and stretching upward to her full height of a tad over five feet. "I suppose that rabbit is supper."

"That and a little fried hoe cake. Hungry?" Monroe smiled.

Mercy, but he had a beautiful smile. Her heart flopped around for a moment like a big catfish landed on the side of the river. Hunger, that's what it was. A pure case of starvation and heat. Douglass would never be infatuated by a man again.

"I'm starving," she said. "Want me to skin the rabbit or take care of the horse?"

"You can skin a rabbit?" he asked incredulously.

"Sure, if you trust me with a knife. I told you I have six brothers, all scattered seven ways to Sunday, of course." She crossed her fingers behind her back. "I can skin a squirrel faster than any of my brothers but Colum can beat me for time when it comes to rabbits. Which do you want me to do?" she asked again.

"You know how to take a saddle off and rub down a horse?" He raised a dark eyebrow and looked down at her. He wasn't a tall man, five feet eight inches if he stretched, but he felt like he was at least six feet tall beside her petite size.

"Grew up on a horse ranch. Momma's people had it for a hundred years I guess. Then Daddy came from Ireland and Grandpa hired him. He knew horses as well as Momma did. They fell in love and Grandpa built them a house on the ranch. Yes, I can take care of the horse and mule if you want to cook tonight."

"Okay. My horse might be a little skittish. He doesn't like anyone but me." Monroe almost chuckled. His horse would give her fits and he'd be willing to bet all that Irish temper would rise to the top by the time she figured out she couldn't take the saddle off or give him a rub down. Yes, he would cook the rabbit and make a skillet of bread, but he'd also take care of his horse, because raised on a horse ranch or not, she wouldn't have any luck with his big black horse Stony.

Monroe unloaded the saddle bags from the pack mule's back and brought out a camping kit. The woman was lying. She'd talked about her Momma and the ranch in Texas like she'd just left it, which she probably had. And he'd be willing to bet dollars to cow patties that her brothers would be coming to see if she married the man she'd left with. Monroe Hamilton wasn't a fool; he could spot a lie a hundred miles away. He'd take her to the nearest town and protect her like she was his own sister, but he'd be darn glad to settle her down in a hotel to wait for her brothers.

Douglass fluffed her wrinkled skirt tails down around her riding boots and watched Monroe for a moment. The knife he unsheathed had a long, skinny blade and Douglass envisioned it for a moment buried all the way to the hilt in Raymond's wickedly deceivious heart. That idea quickly escaped when she reached for the horse's reins and he rolled his eyes and began to back up.

"Ah, you are a skittish critter." She smiled. And no doubt about it, Monroe Hamilton knew it when he let her have the job. Well, she'd show that man where her talents were. "Here, sweet baby boy," she crooned sweetly as she approached the horse. She ran her hands over his muscular neck and tiptoed to pat the top of his head. His eyes stopped rolling but she could still feel the tension bunched in his taut muscles.

Monroe watched Douglass out of the corner of his eye as he skinned the rabbit and cut it up into pieces for frying. She might sweet-talk herself into touching Stony, but she'd never unsaddle him. He'd be willing to bet his half of supper on it.

She tugged on the reins, all the while talking gently to the horse. When his ear was close enough to her face that she could whisper into it, she told him what a beautiful animal he was. Monroe shaved four thin strips of bacon into the skillet he'd set on an iron rack above the fire. He waited until the bacon was thoroughly rendered and enough fat covered the bottom of the skillet to fry a rabbit. He pulled a cloth bag of flour from the supply bag, dumped a little into a tin plate and rolled the rabbit in it, dropping each piece into the sizzling grease.

Douglass still talked to his horse.

Stony nuzzled her neck when she finished whatever she was saying. Was she a witch? He'd heard of people who could tame a wild horse by speaking magic right into their ears, but he'd never thought they came in the form of a slight woman with clear blue eyes and skin the color of lightly creamed coffee.

She kept up a running mumble that he couldn't understand while she removed the saddle and rubbed Stony down with handfuls of grass. The horse even acted like he enjoyed her small hands working on his tired muscles. Monroe's eyes were two slits beneath heavy dark lashes as he cooked the rabbit to perfection, stirred a little water into a cup of flour, along with some salt and soda, and smoothed it out into the skillet to fry for hoe cakes. Monroe grimaced. The horse was a traitor and he had been a fool to let that witch woman near him.

"My job is done," Douglass said when she finished unloading the pack mule's baggage and tethering it to a stake so it could feed upon the green grass. "You got a good horse there, Mr. Hamilton."

"Monroe will do fine," he replied.

"Oh, is your horse named after you?" she asked.

"No, his name is Stony. You can call *me* Monroe. Everytime someone says Mr. Hamilton I expect to see my father standing behind me."

"I see. Why's his name Stony?"

"When the military issued him to me he was as hardheaded as a big field stone out there in the middle of the farm in Love's Valley. Took me weeks to win his trust and to train him, but he's been a good horse. Took me through some fierce battles. Supper is done. Come and get your share."

Douglass watched Monroe closely. He looked to be bonetired and sleepy. Almost as sleepy as she was, but he would rest easy tonight. She sighed at the prospect of another long night with no sleep. She'd barely dozed the night before in the hotel room; she'd been terrified of really going to sleep for fear she'd wake up to find Raymond also awake. It was worth denying herself a few hours of comfort to put days between her and her brothers, though. By the time Monroe awoke at daybreak tomorrow, she'd be long gone, down the road, and Captain Monroe Hamilton would find himself with only a pack mule. He might decide to catch the next coach after all, once he figured out how uncomfortable riding all day bareback could be.

Douglass shut her eyes then opened them wide again. What was she doing? She shouldn't even be pretending to be asleep with a Yankee stranger not ten feet away from her. She stared at the stars for several minutes. He didn't have to escort her to the nearest town. He hadn't been anything but a gentleman, so she had no reason not to trust him. Except he was a Yankee and a man. But still, there was something down deep in her soul that said she was in no danger with Captain Monroe Hamilton. She'd never forget the generosity and kindness Monroe had shown her. It was too bad she had to take his prized horse away from him, but that couldn't be helped.

It was past midnight when her eyes popped open again. She hadn't planned to sleep at all, much less that long. However, she could hear Monroe snoring loud enough to wake the dead, so she doubted she would have a problem with her get-away plan. She saddled the horse as he nuzzled her face, then simply led him quietly out into the darkness. When the snores subsided and all she could hear were crickets and bull frogs, she stuck a booted foot into the stirrup, slung herself into the saddle, and took off at a fast trot.

Daylight came and she slowed down to a steady walk. The horse would be tuckered out by evening if she didn't stop and let him rest a spell. She'd already ridden ten, maybe even fifteen, miles since she left Monroe in his dreams. Considering all he had was a well-laden pack mule to ride after her, she figured a short resting time wouldn't be dangerous. She'd succeeded in her escape and now nothing could go wrong. She would ride west part of the morning, cut back south for a couple of hours, then head east.

Somewhere out there where the sun came up in the morning was a town called Philadelphia. That was her ultimate destination, if her brothers really did believe the note she'd penned that morning before she ran away with Raymond.

Douglass smelled the water before they arrived at the edge of a lake. It looked too wide to make a horse swim across it, she thought, so they'd have to go around it. However, before they did, she fully well intended to have a bath. Thirty minutes wouldn't bring Monroe riding in like the devil was licking his ears. She'd be surprised if the man had even opened his eyes yet.

She tethered Stony to a sapling, giving him enough rope to nibble the grass. She took all the pins from the bun at the nape of her neck, laid them in a neat pile on a rock, and peeled out of her pink dress, leaving it and the petticoats in a pile at the edge of the lake. The water was chilly but not cold, so she dived toward a section of darker-colored water and got wet all over.

She sighed. It seemed like years, not days, since she'd lingered in a bath in her room at the ranch house. She wished for a bar of her own gardenia-scented soap. Every detail of her room came back to haunt her as she cleaned the sweat from her body with the cool, clean water; especially the little desk where she'd hurriedly written a note to her parents, telling them that she was leaving with Raymond Pierce.

Dear Daddy and Momma:
I'm going with Raymond to Philadelphia. Please be happy for me. I love you all, Esmie

She hadn't actually said they were getting married, had she? Her mind, tired from lack of sleep, was a complete muddle. She'd have to sort it out later when she could think clearly. She crawled out of the water, shook herself as best she could, and sat down on a warm rock to let her drawers and camisole dry before she redressed. At least those things touching her skin would be clean even if her dress was beginning to look the worse for wear.

The morning sun warmed her skin, and made her tired eyelids heavy. *Maybe,* she thought, *I will stretch out under that oak tree and rest my eyes. Twenty minutes, no more, and then I'll get dressed and be on my way.*

She'd no more than shut her eyes when she heard gruff masculine voices. They had come to find her! She was glad down deep inside her heart. Her father might rant and rave but she'd talk him out of going to the convent. Maybe even that was only a figment in her imagination and had never been an idea in her father's thinking at all. Maybe Cousin Bertha had *wanted* to go to the convent. Maybe she'd even been abducted instead of eloping. Douglass had just been a little girl when all that happened and she could have very easily gotten the whole story wrong.

She hoped they hadn't hurt Monroe when they found him back there at the campsite with only a mule. He'd been nice man, especially for a Yankee. Douglass eagerly opened one eye to see how many of her brothers her father had sent to bring her back to the ranch.

"Ah, Her Majesty awakens," one man said.

Both blue eyes shot open in spite of her resolve not to look at her brothers. Two burly, dirty men—strangers, both—were staring down at her with evil pouring from their eyes and malicious intent written clearly upon their unshaved faces.

"Who are you?" she asked, wondering how on earth she'd ever get to her dress pocket to retrieve her gun.

"Don't matter who we are. We're going to steal your horse and take you with us," one man said. "Been a long time since we had a woman to cook for us and warm our bed. Looks like we done found us one."

"No, you are not!" Douglass mustered enough courage to stand up. Her mother would be truly mortified if she could see her only daughter parading across the lawn in her unmentionables with two highway robbers looking on. "You're going to get out of here and I mean right now."

"Why, she talks like she's some kind of queen for sure, orderin' us around," one of the men said. "Her Majesty wants us to walk away from a good horse and a fine woman. Get her, Slim. Don't let her near her clothes or that horse."

Monroe awoke in the blink of an eye, knowing intuitively that something was desperately wrong. When his eyes finally adjusted to the darkness, he realized that his horse and Douglass Sullivan were both gone. He jumped up, slapped his thigh so hard it stung and began to shout even louder than he'd snored. He hurriedly loaded his supplies onto the pack mule and picked up the lead reins. He cut a wide circle around the camp and finally picked up Stony's trail headed west. Of all the stupid things; the woman had no intention of going east to send a telegram. Why, any thieving woman who'd steal a man's horse had probably lied about the whole affair of being left beside the road by a rogue who'd shamelessly misled her. Monroe slung a leg over the back of the mule and kicked him. He hugged the animal with his knees until they ached.

Why on earth would Douglass be headed west? he wondered. No doubt, he reassured himself repeatedly, she didn't have six brothers and her name wasn't even Douglass either. After years of being known as the coolest head in the Union Army, he'd been suckered by a bit of fluff with blue eyes. After an hour he stopped and checked the trail again. The horse dung was fresh, still warm, so she was probably no more than an hour ahead of him. He winced as he slung himself back up on the pack mule. He'd drag her to the nearest town and watch while they slipped the noose around her neck and hung her from the gallows. He didn't even care if she was a woman. Gender played no part in it. She was a horse thief.

At sunup he allowed the mule a ten minute rest and himself a chunk of jerky. Rage still filled his belly enough that he didn't eat much. He easily picked up the trail again. No more than a mile farther, she'd turned the horse down a dry creek bed. At the edge of a beautiful lake he found signs of a struggle, and pieces of the lace from the bottom of her petticoat floating from the branches of a shrub. There on a rock beside the water was a whole pile of hair pins. The biggest scuffles seemed to be under the tree where the grass was flattened out and between there and the place where she'd staked Stony. She must have fallen asleep and someone came along and kidnapped her and stole his horse, he figured. During the entire war Stony had never been stolen, and now twice in one day. And all because of a Southern woman.

He fumed as he studied the area carefully. One horse had ridden up to the lake; two from the west joined it; three went on together to the south. Stony left deeper prints going out than he did coming in, so that meant someone much heavier than Douglass was riding him when they left. Monroe wondered how in the world they'd ever mounted him. Douglass was the only other person Stony had ever taken to. Whoever it was had better hope they didn't harm a hair on Stony's body, or Monroe would watch him hang right along with Douglass Sullivan.

He followed the trail all day, staying about an hour behind them by his calculations. At nightfall he finally caught up to them. He heard the ruckus long before he and the mule found the campsite. He tied the mule in the middle of a grove of pecan trees, took his gun from the holster, and crept several hundred yards through the darkness toward the spiraling smoke and bickering voices.

"You lay a hand on me and my brother will draw and quarter you!" Douglass was backed against a tree with one of the men advancing slowly. Any fool could tell exactly what he had in mind.

Good enough for a horse thief, Monroe thought, then quickly chastised himself for thinking that about a woman.

How would he feel if it were his sister in such a predicament? Indigo would not steal a man's horse after he'd extended a helping hand, though. She'd been raised to be a lady and would never be gallivanting around the countryside unescorted in the first place.

"You better be still, woman," the man said gruffly as he made a grab for Douglass.

She sent him back a couple of steps when she raked her fingernails across his face, bringing four lines of blood dripping down onto his shirt collar.

"I said for you to stay away from me," she threatened through clenched teeth.

"Need some help taming her?" the second man asked from the campfire. "Want me to hold her down, Slim?"

"Naw, she's goin' to pay for this," Slim replied.

Monroe whistled softly and Stony lifted his tired head from the stake where he'd been tied. Douglass caught the movement and looked into the darkness. Surely, Monroe wasn't out there. That mule couldn't cover so much ground so quickly.

"So you goin' to be still or am I goin' to tie you up?" Slim asked.

"That horse you stole belongs to my brother and he only raises his head up like that when he smells his master. You had better think twice before you tie me up. My brother will tear your heart out with his bare hands and feed it to the buzzards," Douglass said, trying her best not to appear afraid. Her knees shook beneath her petticoats so badly she could hear them knocking together, but she had to keep bluffing. Colum said she was ninety percent bluff and only ten percent mean. Flannon always said he didn't want to be on the other end of the mean if the bluff failed. Perhaps she could bluff her way out of this yet, especially if Stony would keep looking off out there in the darkness at some mockingbird with insomnia.

"Hello camp," Monroe sang out as he walked right in among them.

"Monroe!" Douglass ran past the wicked man with the brown teeth and beady little eyes and into his arms. "Kill them both."

"Now why should I do that, little sister?" Monroe laughed, playing along with the game she'd started. "You ran away from home so this is your party. Which one of these fellers is your husband? Or did they kidnap you right out of your bed?"

"Neither one of us," one of the men answered. "We ain't about to marry nobody. And we didn't kidnap her out of a bed neither. She was sleeping under a tree."

"Oh?" Monroe brought his gun up so fast both men wondered where it had come from. "You mean you have ruined my sister's reputation and you don't intend to make an honest woman of her. Well, one of you is going to marry her. We'll ride on into the nearest town and one of you can stand right up before the judge and say 'I do' or I'll just shoot both of you right now."

"Hey man, we found her back there by a little lake. Woman shouldn't be out in the open alone like that if she don't want to get into trouble. We didn't know she was anybody's sister," Slim whined.

"Well?" Monroe looked at Douglass who'd backed away from his embrace as soon as the gun appeared. "I don't know. Our father isn't going to want her back. She's damaged goods. No one in the whole eastern half of Texas is going to want her now. How about I sell her to you?" he asked.

"Monroe!" Douglass protested, slapping at his face.

He caught her small hand in his and held it tightly, amazed at the tingle he felt when her skin touched his. "Don't you hit me, Douglass. You ain't worth much now but I might make a few dollars off of you even if you are a horse thief," he growled. "What would you two give me for her?"

"God Almighty, I ain't buyin' that she-cat." The man by the fire stood up and scratched his head. "I'd give you all the

money in my saddle bag for that horse but I wouldn't give a
plug nickel for the woman. If I got to pay for a woman I sure
don't want to have to tame her first. And that one thinks
she's a queen or something. Take forever to get that out of
her."

"Horse ain't for sale, woman is," Monroe said.

"Then there ain't no sale goin' on today," the man replied.

"Then I'll be taking my horse and this woman and riding
on out of here. If you're sure you don't want to either marry
her or buy her, I'll take her on with me. We'll make
arrangements to put her in a nunnery next week," Monroe
said, grabbing Douglass' arm and leading her backward
toward Stony. He didn't trust these two bandits any farther
than he could throw their sorry hides.

"Good place for the likes of her. Thinks she's some kind
of royalty or something. Ain't nothing but a half-breed
Mexican. She musta had a different Momma than you got.
Ain't one thing about you two that looks alike. Just get her
on out of here. Sure you don't want to sell that horse?"

"No, sir. Horse is my best friend. I'd sell the woman, but
not the horse," Monroe said, wondering how in the world he
was going to saddle the horse and hold the highway bandits
off with only two hands. To give Douglass the gun would be
sheer lunacy. To leave behind the saddle and ride bareback
would be misery, and besides, he'd worn that saddle in to fit
him perfectly. He wasn't leaving it behind. Trusting a lying
woman, though, took every ounce of will power he could
conjure up.

"Keep them right where they are," he growled as he handed Douglass the gun and saddled up Stony.

Six bullets, Douglass noticed. She could kill all three of
them and have three to spare. Selling her to those filthy crea-
tures; a hot fury filled her breast at the very idea. She'd shoot
Monroe first, right between those pretty brown eyes. Then
she'd take out the nearest horse thief and before he hit the
ground, the other one would be joining him. They could all

three explain to St. Peter why they were marching up to the Pearly Gates together. She hoped he gave them a first class ticket straight to hell.

"Well, Douglass?" Monroe said when he was in the saddle, an outstretched hand toward her. Relunctantly, she handed him the gun, took his hand, settled into the saddle behind him, and wrapped her arms around his strong chest. Several bullets cut through the air around them as the two men hurriedly retrieved their guns and put up one last effort to have the horse. She buried herself against Monroe's back and swallowed the screams begging to rush out of her throat. She held her breath so long he began to wonder if she'd been shot and was already dead, but after a while he felt her shudder as she sucked enough Texas air into her lungs to keep them from exploding.

"We've got to ride part of the night to put some distance between us and those highway pirates. You'll stay awake and you won't cause any more trouble or I'm going to kick you off the back of this horse and leave you for them to fight over."

"I can ride the mule," she said.

"Sure you can, but I don't have time to be looking back over my shoulder to see if you've stolen my mule and all my supplies. No, ma'am, you are riding on this horse with me tonight. I'm of a mind to give you to the sheriff for horse thievery at the next town we come to. That was a mighty ugly trick you pulled. I was trying to help you."

Douglass bit her lower lip and held back the sass. It wasn't an easy feat but she managed, infuriating Monroe all the more. If he did give her to the sheriff, they might hang her, or, worse yet, put her in jail until her identity could be proven if her family ever tracked her down. She had a sneaking suspicion that the hanging might be the lesser of the two evils.

Monroe studied the situation slowly and methodically for the better part of an hour after he'd grabbed the reins to the pack mule without unmounting. To leave her in a town would be sheer folly. To take her with him would be worse than folly. Either way he was doomed.

"I've decided to take you with me," he finally announced through gritted teeth and with a weary voice as he pulled up under the shadows of a big elm tree and dismounted to rest the horse for a few minutes. "I will escort you all the way to Philadelphia because that's what a gentleman should do. I'm not sure I believe you though, Douglass Sullivan. I think you are lying to me, but I'm not leaving you on your own. You said you were going to Philadelphia to visit an aunt. I've got a feeling that part could be true. I think you must be telling the truth about the escort treating you shamelessly. Could be you were eloping and found out too late you'd trusted the wrong man, but I'll give you enough credit to think you wouldn't do that. But I don't think you are an orphan for one minute, lady, so you can stop that pretense. One more horse stealing stunt though and I'll leave you behind so fast you'll wonder if you ever met a Yankee captain who hasn't much sense if he's willing to escort you anywhere."

"I'm stopping at the next town," Douglass replied. That much time in the company of a man who'd been willing to sell her to those vile men was more than the Good Lord would expect of her, even if she had stolen his horse. No sir. She was going to get a room in an inn and telegraph home. Her father would send someone for her. Even having to face her oldest brother's temper wouldn't be as dreadful as riding all the way to some horrid Yankee state with this man.

"Then you can stay right here and fight with those two men," Monroe said, grabbing the mule's lead rope and hoisting his tired body back into the saddle on Stony's back. He hated the thought of riding all night, but when they came to a town, he'd rent a room, tie her to the bed, and get some real sleep.

Douglass took the proffered hand for the second time that night and swung herself back up behind Monroe. By the time morning came, she thought, she'd never walk like a lady again. She'd be bowlegged the rest of her natural days. *Nuns don't care,* her conscience reminded her bluntly. *The black habit will cover up your bowed legs.*

The moon was a big white ball floating on a bed of twinkling stars when she shut her eyes and sagged against his back. In a few seconds she jerked herself awake and straightened her back, ramrod stiff.

"You can nap if you want," Monroe said bluntly, no warmth in his voice.

To be honest, Douglass didn't blame him one bit. There he was riding home after fighting all those years in the war and then spending a whole year in Texas, and suddenly he finds himself strapped with a damsel in distress. The only gentlemanly thing to do was rescue her, then she had reciprocated by stealing his horse. She shot her chin up in defiance even though he didn't have eyes in the back of his head to see the gesture. It was the third night she'd gone without sleep, but she wasn't going to let the steady motion of the horse lull her to sleep. If he could stay awake so could she.

"Hey, you see what I see? That's a town up there. Maybe there are rooms above the saloon. I could sleep a week," he said.

A bed, she considered with a sigh. *A real one with a feather mattress and maybe even a wash bowl and pitcher. Luxury deluxe.*

"Can I trust you, Douglass?" Monroe asked as they rode up to the saloon.

"Just get me a room," she responded shortly. "I'm too tired to run away, and I'm sure Stony is too tired to even carry me anywhere. We'll decide tomorrow whether I'm going with you or staying right here."

"Oh, you are going with me all the way to Philadelphia where I'll deliver you to your aunt who had the misfortune to marry a Yankee all those years ago. It's the only way I can trust you. If I leave you behind, you could easily persuade the sheriff to arrest me on kidnapping charges or worse. I have not stayed alive in this whole war just to finish my time and face a hangman's noose for bogus charges. I already know you are capable of lying and stealing, so you are coming to Philadelphia, lady. I'll deliver you into the hands of your poor little aunt who has no idea what kind of niece she has," he said without a hint of humor. What a mess he'd gotten himself into, he thought, but he was wise enough to know that keeping Douglass with him and pretending to be her escort would have far fewer repercussions than if she went howling that she'd been abducted by a Yankee while he was still in uneasy Rebel territory.

I'll accompany you as long as it suits me and not a minute longer, Douglass thought, her nod depleting all her energy. *Horse stealing ain't all of my charms, Captain.*

Chapter Four

Monroe was surprised to see a light on in the saloon, then even more amazed that the bartender was still sweeping up the floor. "Evenin', sir," he said, pushing the doors open and dragging Douglass inside by her hand.

"Closed up for the night," the bartender said. "Can't even offer you a whiskey. Done sold out and can't get no more for two days."

"I'm not lookin' for a drink, but a couple of rooms," Monroe replied.

"Got one, but not two. You lookin' for work?" He eyed Douglass carefully. She could be a beauty if someone taught her how to fix that straggling mop of black hair and wash her face.

"No, she isn't," Monroe answered before she had time to speak her mind. "This is my cousin. She was abducted and I've rescued her. We are on our way back home to Pennsylvania. I'll take that room if you'd rent it out."

"Might as well. Third door on the left," the barkeep said with a nod up the stairs. "Dollar for the night."

Monroe took a coin from his pocket and handed it to the fellow. "Got a livery in town?"

"Sure, down at the end of the street. Sampson has done gone to bed, so pick out a stall. You can pay him in the mornin' when you go claim the livestock."

"Thank you," Monroe said politely before he led

Douglass up the stairs. "I'm going to unload my bags and bring in the ones with your personal things. Then I'm taking the horse and mule to the livery. Promise me that I can trust you?"

She looked around the room. A bed was pushed against the far wall. She didn't care if Monroe slept in the stable with the horses, that bed belonged to her tonight. In the corner she saw a washstand with towels draped over the rod and water in the pitcher. It didn't matter if it was cold as clabber or lukewarm, she would wash up before she passed out between those patched sheets. Nothing had ever looked so good to her in her entire life.

"Answer me," Monroe insisted.

"Yes, you can trust me. I'm so exhausted I'll be asleep before you get back," she said, tiredness oozing out between the words as she spoke. She didn't even wince when she heard him lock her in the room. If she had wanted to escape, a locked door wouldn't keep her from it.

A few minutes later, the door opened a crack and Monroe shoved two saddle bags inside the room. Then it shut carefully and she heard him lock it again. She'd already begun to unbutton the front of her dress by the time she heard his boots on the stairs. She stepped out of her beautiful pink dress, letting it puddle up at her feet. The hem had been ripped in several places, dirt stains covered the entire skirt, and one sleeve hung by a thread. She'd do the best she could until tomorrow morning, then she'd see if this little town had a general store where she could perhaps purchase a dress or a good riding habit. If not, then a spool of thread and a needle so she could do a major repair job.

She retrieved her comb and brush from the saddle bags, as well as a change of underthings. She rushed through the rest of her bath and slipped into white drawers and a matching camisole, then she carefully washed the set she'd been wearing and hung them over the end of the bed to dry. She brushed the knots from her long black hair and braided it

into two ropes that hung to her hips. Retrieving some of the
hair from her brush, she wove it around and around the ends
of the braids to keep them from coming loose. Turning back
the sheets, she checked the bed carefully. Although the
sheets wore patches, they smelled clean and fresh. Her eyes
were shut by the time her head carved out a place in the
feather pillow.

Monroe knocked gently on the door. When he got no
answer he hurriedly opened it, half expecting to see an
empty room. True to her word, Douglass was curled up in a
ball on the back side of the bed. A gentle breeze flowed
through the open window, fanning the thin floral curtains
until they practically brushed her nose, but it would take
more than the touch of fabric on her face to wake Douglass.

Monroe propped his elbows on the footboard of the bed,
being careful not to lean his dirty hands on her clean clothing, and stared his fill. She'd tossed the top sheet away from
her body, and the cotton undergarments did little to conceal
her curves. An ample high bosom rested on a small rib cage,
drawers were laced with a pink ribbon around a waist he
could circle completely with his big hands. She lay curled on
her side, the curve of her hips silhouetted against the moonlit window. Two long braids draped over one shoulder and
one drooped off the side of the bed. Monroe reached out and
carefully raised it off the floor.

Douglass Sullivan was a lovely young lady. A stirring
deep in the pit of his soul caused him to shake his head, as
if the gesture would erase the feelings. He'd sworn he would
never fall in love, and he'd live with that vow. Not even a
beautiful woman clad only in her underwear could claw
through the thick layer of elephant skin around his heart.

She'd left half the water in the pitcher, but had failed to
discard the dirty water in the bowl. He sat down in a straight
back chair and removed his boots and socks, then picked up
the bowl and tossed its contents out the window. Suspenders
unhitched, he began his own clean-up, working his way

down from his face, across the broad expanse of his muscular chest, and ending with his feet. He threw his own dirty water out the window and kicked a saddle bag over in the corner to serve as a pillow.

But, oh, that bed did look inviting. He gazed at it a long time, his eyelids getting heavier and harder to keep open. "She'll never know," whispered as he eased his body carefully on the bed beside Douglass. If she awoke and put up a fuss, he'd be the gentleman and sleep on the floor, but if she didn't . . . ah, but the real pillow felt like heavenly clouds beneath his head. He wiggled his way into a comfortable position, very careful not to touch Douglass, and sighed once before he fell sleep.

It seemed they'd only been asleep a few minutes when a high-pitched feminine voice woke them with a shake of the bedstead and a giggle. "Hey you two lovebirds?" She giggled again.

Douglass purred like a kitten, expecting to see the ranch maid when she opened her eyes. She hugged up the big pillow tight against her and thought she'd wait one more minute before starting the day. When she opened her eyes she found what she thought was a pillow was really Monroe Hamilton. He had one arm under her and the other thrown around her, drawing her tightly to him.

Monroe's eyes fluttered open long enough for the bright sun to penetrate. He withdrew his hand from around the pillow he'd snuggled up against, to shade his eyes from the rude intrusion. Why hadn't his sister Indigo wakened him earlier? He'd told her last night before he went to bed that he needed to check the corn crop today. One more second and he'd throw back the covers. He opened his eyes lazily to find a woman in his arms. Where was he and what had he done?

"Hey, Jasper says you and your cousin paid for a room for a night, and it's noon. Says if you ain't goin' to be out in an hour, then he's going to charge you another dollar," the lady said.

Douglass jumped away from the man next to her. Monroe sat straight up and pulled the sheet up to cover his bare chest. Sun streamed through the window and the woman standing beside the bed grinned like a possum eating grapes through a barbed wire fence.

"Cousin, huh? Well, maybe a kissin' cousin," the woman said with a giggle. "You're 'bout a pretty little thing. Jasper said you would be if you got cleaned up. Reckon you'd want to stay on and keep this room? We're needin' another girl around here. Got more business than me and the other three can take care of."

"No!" Douglass jumped out of the bed, trying to shake the warmth of Monroe's arm flung around her sleeping body from her skin, without any luck.

"Well, don't get huffy," the woman said. "Like I said, ya'll got an hour or you'll have to pay up with Jasper."

"We're in a brothel," Douglass exclaimed incredulously when the woman slammed the door behind her. "Patrick would die if he knew I'd slept in a brothel. Oh, my lord, he's going to kill us both. I told you I was sleeping in the bed and you could have the floor. What are you doing in the bed?"

"Patrick? That one of your brothers that's been scattered seven ways to Sunday? You are lying to me Douglass Sullivan, if that's really even your name. And what was I doing in your bed? Sleeping." He chuckled. "Trust me, I was only sleeping. That's all I was doing. Besides there's nothing about you that appeals to me, so don't worry, I won't try to take advantage of you, Douglass."

"You are a rapscallion," she fumed, stepping into her petticoats.

"Don't put those on," he told her as he swung his feet onto the floor and stood up, stretching to his full height and working the kinks out of his muscles. "I'm going to make a trip to the general store and purchase you some clothing fit for riding. Then I'm going to the livery and buy a horse if they have one for sale. I should be back in less than an hour. I don't suppose you'll run away in your underwear?"

"Get out!" As the door slammed shut she turned her back and stared out the window at the small town hustle and bustle already going on. Directly across the street was a bank with a general store on one side and a milliner on the other. She could see two gorgeous hats in the window, both with lace and feathers. She'd just about give everything in her money bag for one of those hats, she thought as she watched people coming and going. Last week, she'd been one of those people in her own little town. How things did change in a moment.

"Gentleman paid for your breakfast." The lady who'd awakened them kicked the door open and brought in a tray with toast and coffee on it. "He said to stay right here with you and make sure you ate every bite. Something about it being a while until nightfall and supper. Want to talk to old Lizzy about what's going on here?"

"No, I don't," Douglass said shortly. "I'm sorry. It's a long story and . . ."

"Ain't they all." Lizzy laughed. "I'll be over across the hallway if you change your mind, honey. Let me tell you something. If he ain't your cousin, then you make him marry you. He's done ruined you, sleeping in the same bed with you like that. He's a looker that one is, but he seems like a decent feller."

Douglass nodded and bit into the toast. There was no going back now. The sheriff wouldn't believe she'd been kidnapped with Lizzy telling what she'd seen.

She ate every crumb of the thick-sliced, pan-fried bread, relishing every bite, and drank two cups of strong black coffee while she watched the people from the window. She unbraided her hair and brushed it, wishing she'd told Monroe to bring her a handful of hair pins. There was money in her sack to pay for them, she reasoned when her conscience reminded her that she shouldn't ask a stranger for a favor.

Even if she had spent the night curled up in his strong arms.

Monroe Hamilton was a handsome man. From the window she watched him tip his hat to a lady on the wooden sidewalk outside the general store. He carried a parcel tied in brown paper close to his body as he walked up the street to the livery. Even if he wasn't the man for Douglass, she could still be honest and admit that he was easy on the eyes. As two women passed him and turned back for a second look Douglass felt high color filling her cheeks. She'd been looking at him the same way.

He led a pretty little butternut-colored filly from the livery, along with Stony and the pack mule, and tied all three to the hitching post outside the saloon. Douglass could hear his deep resonant voice exchange a few words with the bartender, and then halfway up the stairs, his steps ceased and she heard a high pitched giggle. Did all women react to him the same way? How in the world had he remained single?

Monroe didn't bother to knock on the door, but barged right in. Douglass was sitting in the straight back chair, her long black hair almost reaching the floor.

"There's a pair of britches and a shirt. Be a whole lot more comfortable for riding. We'll buy you a dress when we get closer to Philadelphia or when we decide to ride the stagecoaches. I wouldn't expect you to wear britches in those instances. I found a good horse but the man didn't have a lady's saddle so it's a good thing I bought boy's clothing for you. The saddle is one a young man outgrew. I think the stirrups are even about the right length." He paused and glanced at her legs.

A slow heat crept up the back of her neck and scorched her cheeks. "You can sit in this chair and face the wall," she said.

"Why? I figured you'd put the pants and shirt on over top of your unmentionables." He grinned. "And I forgot, I picked these up on a rock beside the creek where those men grabbed you." He laid a fistful of hairpins on the washstand.

Douglass set her mouth in a firm line and picked up the parcel he'd tossed on the bed—a pair of dun-colored britches and a shirt of the same fabric. She tugged the pants on over her drawers and was amazed at how well they fit. The shirt was a little long but she shoved the tails down into the pants and drew a leather belt through the loops. She felt like she did when she was a little girl and played dress-up in Flannon's outgrown boy's clothes.

"I don't even get a thank you?" Monroe sat down in the chair and leaned back until the front two legs were in the air and the back slats of the chair were against the wall. "Send up breakfast. Retrieve your hair pins. Buy you clothing and a horse."

"Seems like a small price to pay for ruining my reputation last night," she said, twisting two long braids into a crown on top of her head and securing it tightly with the pins. Before they left she fully intended to go to that general store herself and buy a hat; a great big sombrero, if they had one.

"Hey, your reputation was already ruined. Now mine is," he said, a broad grin covering his face. "Are you going to marry me so my mother doesn't send me to a convent?"

"I'm not your type, remember? And Captain Hamilton, I do not intend to tell a single soul that you slept in *my* bed last night," she said. "You better get those saddle bags or else find another dollar. I think our hour is about up."

"Yes, ma'am." The grin faded. She wasn't his type. That was a fact that could be written in history books. He was a Hamilton of Love's Valley, Pennsylvania, and he'd stand by his promise to take her to Philadelphia. Hamiltons always kept their word. That he was taking her to Philadelphia because he didn't want to be branded a kidnapper or whatever else she might decide to charge him with was beside the point. He would stand beside his word, but he'd bet his boots and spurs that the journey was going to keep him on his toes.

* * *

The sun, a big orange ball, hung low on the far horizon when Monroe and Douglass found an abandoned, burned out homestead several miles north of a little town called Friendship, Arkansas. If their luck held, they'd make it to North Little Rock by the next night and perhaps board a stagecoach for the next leg of the journey. Monroe had papers to pick up in North Little Rock, Memphis, Nashville, Knoxville, and Richmond. When he'd delivered them by hand to President Johnson himself, in Washington D.C., then he would be free and could go home to Love's Valley. He dismounted without asking Douglass if she'd like to stop for the day. He picked up a charred log and smelled it, then sniffed the air. "No smoke in the wind, but this place hasn't been burned for more than a week," he commented without expecting an answer.

He wasn't disappointed.

Douglass' heart went out to the people who'd lost their home and she hoped that it was due to the lady of the house leaving a skillet of grease on the stove and not some marauders who'd murdered the whole family. Before they inspected the site closer, though, she really needed to run down to that little house at the end of the trail behind where the house used to sit. She blushed thinking about Monroe knowing where she was headed, but there didn't seem to be any other recourse. She couldn't very well excuse herself on the pretext of needing to "freshen up." Her bladder was on the verge of exploding, so she swallowed her pride, slid out of the saddle, dropped the reins, and went straight for the outhouse which still stood sturdy and useful at the back of the lot. A few minutes later she emerged and saw the garden she'd passed without even seeing on her way to relieve herself. She came close to dancing a jig when she found over-ripe tomatoes on the vine, potatoes and carrots under the ground, and squash hiding from the sun under big green leaves.

"Tonight I cook. I found the garden," she yelled at

Monroe who was still wandering around the burned house. "You take care of the horses. Please tell me you didn't find anyone in all that burned rubble."

He shook his head. There were no skeletons, so the people who lived here must have survived the fire. He thought of his aunt and uncle who hadn't survived a fire when the Rebels burned their house to the ground. Ellie wouldn't have either if she had been home instead of visiting with Monroe's mother and sister in Love's Valley.

A charred cookstove told him where the kitchen must have been and the remnants of an old iron bedstead, much like the one he and Douglass shared the night before, meant that he stood where a bedroom had been. Did these folks have children? Did they weep when they had to leave their home and garden? He shrugged off the mounting depression and led the horses to the barn where he found stables, a loft full of hay, and a roof to sleep under.

"Where's the camp gear?" Douglass came through the open barn doors with her hands full of red tomatoes and yellow squash. "And is there a hoe or a shovel left in here so I can dig potatoes? I can pull up the carrots and onions with my bare hands, but I can't get the potatoes up. Reckon there's still a well?"

"This might work." He tossed a pitchfork toward her, careful not to hit her with it. She caught it in her left hand and didn't even drop a tomato.

Good reflexes, he thought.

While he took care of the animals, she found the well and brought up a pail of water. She washed vegetables and used the sharp knife to dice them into small pieces. The metal water bucket became a kettle to boil everything together into a soup. If only she had some meat, she'd have a fine supper. But that was stretching a miracle. That they had fresh vegetables and a roof over their heads for the night was more than she'd hoped for when the coffee and two pieces of toast had failed her several hours before.

After Monroe helped Douglass set up the iron rods and

start a fire to set her bucket of water on, he went back into
the barn. He rubbed down both horses and fed them hay
from the loft. Douglass could sleep at one end of the loft
and he'd have the other. He could stretch out and not even
think about whether or not he might touch her. When Stony
and the mule had begun feasting, Monroe climbed the ladder up into the loft again. He used another pitchfork to
make two separate beds, one on each end of the loft.
Whether she liked it or not, she was sleeping on the one
farthest from the loft window. He intended to enjoy whatever night breezes there were on this hot night. He threw
himself down on the pile of hay and laced his hands behind
his head. The smell of vegetables boiling over a campfire
filled his nostrils and made his stomach grumble.

"A good haunch of beef or venison would be nice,"
Douglass mumbled as she sliced another onion and dropped
it into the pot filled with potatoes and carrots. When they
were just shy of done, she'd add squash to the mixture.

"Meat would take hours to boil up tender anyway," she
reminded herself. That quirky little feeling that comes over
a woman when someone, especially a man, is watching her,
suddenly made her skin crawl. Was there someone out there
in the semi-darkness? The people who burned down these
folks' home, perhaps? Or her brothers—heaven help her,
she'd hope for a physical battle with the arsonists over a
mental one with her own kin. She looked at the tall pecan
trees behind the barn. Nothing there. She scanned the rolling
hills off to the north and couldn't see a single thing. Putting
both her hands on the ground, she held her breath. No horse
hooves on the way or she'd be able to feel them in her palms.
Then she looked up to see Monroe lying on his side in the
loft window. She strained her ears and, sure enough, he was
snoring.

Douglass checked the soup pot one more time and went
inside the barn. Butter, her horse, whinnied, begging for
attention, so Douglass took time to whisper in her ear. She
was on her way to the ladder when she heard a pitiful

meow from the other end of the barn. A quick search turned up a mother cat with four baby kittens who'd opened their eyes just recently. She took a few minutes to pet all of them, cuddling each one to her chest and wishing she could take all of them with her. Then she started up the ladder to wake Monroe for supper. By the time he got his eyes open and the frown off his face, the stew should be ready.

She found two bed-sized mounds of hay in the loft. Monroe slept on the one closest to the window. Apparently, the other one was to be her bed for the night. Well, it sure wasn't as comfortable looking as the feather bed had been last night, but it beat the dickens out of the bare ground with saddle bags for pillows. She sat down on the edge of the straw pile. Stars had already began to peep out from behind the midnight-blue curtain of darkness. The aroma of a good vegetable soup wafted through the air. Simple things, to be sure, but life sustaining. She felt a good bit of her indignation sliding away as she inhaled more of the soup scents and thought about those soft baby kittens down in the hay. So many things she'd taken for granted all her life suddenly didn't seem so important anymore.

A soft raspy sound like someone walking gently on paper caused her to stop philosophizing and not move a muscle. Someone was near, sneaking up on them. She eased over to the ladder and looked down into the barn. No one was there. She peeped out the window but the only thing below her was a pot of bubbling stew. Her ears hurt, she listened so hard.

There it was again.

This time she pinned it down to the area on the other side of where Monroe slept. She tiptoed to the edge of the hay mound and leaned forward, her eyes meeting those of a coiled rattlesnake. Instinct, covered with a thick layer of pure fear, overrode everything she'd been thinking. Monroe's pistol was out of the gun belt around his hips and in her hand in an instant. Before the snake could shake his tail again, its head was blown against the wooden barn wall.

Monroe jumped, grabbed his ear, and reached for his gun all at the same time. The people who'd burned out the barn must be back again and this time gunning for blood. Had they already shot Douglass? When he could see past the fog of sleep, he realized she was standing in front of him with his own gun in her hands. Good Lord, had she tried to kill him as he napped?

"What are you doing?" He screamed but couldn't hear his own voice.

Why was she trying to kill him? He'd thought he could trust her after last night. Not one time all day had she tried to run away although the opportunities had been many. He held his ears but the ringing wouldn't stop.

Douglass carefully laid the gun in its rightful place, careful not to touch Monroe. The feelings evoked in her body when she rode behind him, and the warmth of his body next to hers that morning, weren't sensations she wanted to experience again, especially right then, when every nerve in her body was already quivering.

"Snake." She pointed with shaking fingers toward the dead thing not two feet from Monroe's feet.

He could tell she was saying something but he couldn't make out a thing. "Why are you shooting at me?" he screamed.

She shook her head. There'd be a roar in his ears for a little while, but she knew it would cease by the time they had eaten. She walked around him and picked up the snake by the tail. "I asked for meat. Well, be careful what you pray for because you might get it. Thank goodness it's a snake. They cook up real fast." She threw the six-foot rattler out the window.

"Snake!" Monroe yelled as she tossed it out the window.

"Yes, it is," Douglass said with a nod. She climbed down the ladder and was skinning the snake by the time he reached the camp fire.

"What are you doing?" he asked, trying to rub the remaining roar from his ears.

"Supper," she said, pointing to the soup pot.

"No," he replied. "I'm not eating snake."

She smiled brightly. "Yes, you will. It's good meat, tastes like chicken, and it cooks fast." She enunciated slowly so he could understand her.

He was still shaking his head when she cut up the white meat and tossed it in the bucket with the boiling vegetables. Monroe did have a choice: He could eat what she prepared or starve. He'd eaten possum, raccoon, squirrel, groundhog, bread full of mold and weevils, even horse meat during the war when he had been thankful to get anything, so what was the difference?

When she finished tossing pieces of meat into the pot, she took the skin and carefully scraped the backside, then stretched it over the barn door to dry. "Folks might come back. They can make a hat band," she said, again talking slowly and motioning with her hands the whole time.

When the two sat down to eat, the soup was delicious; the best Monroe had eaten in a long time. He wondered if this whole area was covered with rattlesnakes. He could easily develop a taste for the white meat and could imagine it fried with a cornmeal batter covering it. Eventually his ears stopped roaring and started a buzzing sensation, like a hundred bumble bees flying around in his head. By the time they'd put out the campfire and climbed the ladder to their bedroom, even that had almost stopped.

Both of them checked the hay loft carefully before they laid down for the night. Douglass removed her hand-tooled leather boots, gave thanks that she'd opted to wear them rather than her Sunday shoes when she had so very ignorantly run away with Raymond, and laid back in the straw. It seemed a lifetime ago that she had listened to his lies and promises.

Monroe opted to lay as far as he could away from the

remainder of the snake's head on the wall. He knew he'd be in a world of pain right then if Douglass hadn't been such a good shot. And a good cook too, he had to admit.

"So what is your first name?" Her soft southern voice broke through the darkness, and his thoughts.

"What brought that on?" he asked.

"I think shooting the eyeballs out of a six-foot rattler with twelve buttons is pretty close to saving your sorry hide, and when a person saves another's life, then they owe them something. I want to know your name," she said.

"I don't think shooting a snake constitutes saving my life. It might have slithered away and not struck at me at all." he responded.

"Oh, I'm sure that snake was going to kiss you goodnight and tell you a bedtime story. If I'd stopped and thought, I could've saved a bullet. Because if it bit a hard-hearted Yankee it would have died within three minutes anyway," she said shortly.

"We're even, way I see it," he said with a chuckle.

"How's that?" she asked, her tone getting colder by the minute.

"I bought you a horse and a suit of clothing. I even took you back to the store so you could buy that hideous Mexican hat, and you didn't even say thank you. So you killed a snake to keep it from biting me. Guess that makes us even," he said. He'd bet his last dollar that her blue eyes were flashing with a good dose of pure old mad.

"Good night, Mr. Hamilton," she said coldly.

"Good night to you too, Miss Sullivan," he replied curtly.

She flopped over on her side so she didn't even have to look at his form in the moonlit hay loft. If her mother knew she'd been rude to the very man who'd saved her life as well as her virtue, she'd never hear the end of it. But if his mother knew he'd called her on bad manners—even if he was a Yankee and everyone knew they had no manners—she'd probably slap him silly.

Yes, they were even. But it wouldn't be long until she out-did him, and then she'd make him tell her his first name. It must be the most awful thing in the world she thought, if he wouldn't even utter it. She had a smile on her face when she shut her eyes and fell into a deep sleep.

Chapter Five

Douglass slid out of the saddle hoping she never again had to ride that long and hard. It had been more than thirty miles in one day; sun up to past sun down in the saddle, with only a five minute stop at noon for a drink of water from a cool spring and a leftover biscuit from breakfast and a few minutes to rest the horses and let them drink when they'd passed a stream. Sweat, mixed with trail dust, created tiny mud balls in the creases in her neck, and strands of straight black hair stuck to her face like they'd been glued there with flour and water paste.

"I want my own room," she said, following Monroe into the hotel in Benton, Arkansas. "I want a bath and supper brought to the room. I'll pay for all of it myself, please."

"Maybe you'd better emphasize that second word, Douglass," Monroe growled, as tired as she was and perhaps even more ready for a hot meal and a bath.

"Not only do I *want,* I will have," she demanded. "I've got money of my own and you don't have to pay for my keep."

"Hush," he snorted. "Money isn't the issue here."

"Help you?" an older man said from the service desk.

"Yes, we would like two rooms," Monroe said. "With hot baths brought up, and is it too late to have supper in the room?"

"No sir." The man smiled. "Costs extra. Room is a dollar for each one; bath, two bits; and a meal, another dollar to

53

have it brought to the rooms. That'd be four dollars and fifty cents for all of it."

"Fine," Monroe dug into the pocket of his trousers and handed the man a five dollar gold piece. "Keep the change and bring dinner first."

"Yes, sir." The man smiled again. "They had roast beef with vegetables and apple pie for dessert in the dining room for supper. Suppose that would work?"

Douglass clenched her teeth to keep from moaning in delight. Even if the beef was tough as shoe leather and drier than a July day in Texas, she'd eat every bite and not fuss about it. How could she have ever taken so much for granted? she wondered.

Monroe nodded and picked up the two keys the man laid on the desk. Rooms six and seven at the end of the hallway on the second floor. Douglass could have six since seven was Monroe's lucky number, and right then he didn't care one whit if he woke up the next morning to find her gone. The price of a horse, saddle, and a change of clothes would surely be cheap enough to get rid of the snippet of a woman. Though, he did have to admit she'd ridden well that day. Never a cross word or whine and he'd driven them both hard all day. He'd wanted to make Benton by nightfall and by golly, they'd done it. Any other woman, his sister included, would have put up a fuss at sitting a horse for more than thirty miles. He had to give Douglass credit where it was due; the woman certainly had stamina and strength.

Douglass had enough stamina and strength to take the key to room number six from his hand and open the door, yet she barely had enough to shut the door behind her, drop her saddle bags on the floor, and fall into a heap beside them. No way was she even sitting on the bed before she cleaned up. The man was a complete monster to expect a woman to ride those kind of hours and at that speed, but she would have given up the ghost and dropped graveyard dead before she complained about the severity of the ride. Was it going to be like this the whole rest of the trip to Philadelphia? If it was then she'd have double reason to make Raymond swallow his two front teeth and put up with a crooked nose the rest of his life. Everything she had to endure getting to Pennsylvania only added to the force of the blow she intended to deliver to that gutter rat.

By the time she wolfed down a whole platter of roast beef surrounded by carrots, potatoes, and onions, three cold biscuits, and a generous slab of pie, her strength was renewed enough that she figured she could crawl in and out of the oval bathtub the maid had brought up while Douglass ate. The young girl made several trips up and down the stairs filling the tub, her face not able to disguise the disgust she felt at the woman sitting at a tiny table, dressed like a man, and eating like a field hand. Douglass would have smiled at her aversion but she didn't have enough energy. Besides, just last week, she herself would have had the same expression as the maid if she'd seen a woman looking like she did right that moment. Women didn't wear pants. They didn't wolf down their food. They didn't tell lies about having an aunt in Philadelphia just so they could go there to wreak havoc with an abominable Yankee.

You are just as much to blame as he is, her conscience reprimanded her. *You wanted an adventure because your brothers had one in the war. You thought you could elope with Raymond and have an adventure called a honeymoon. You were as much to fault as he was.*

After the last bite of pie, Douglass leaned back and thought through the next few weeks with a more rational mind, one that wasn't plumb starving to death. Raymond wasn't worth the effort it would take to go all the way to Philadelphia. Tomorrow morning she was going to thank the Yankee captain for his help. She would ask for his address so her family could reimburse him for all the money he'd spent and then she was going straight to the telegraph office to send a wire to her father. Her mother might call the nearest convent and offer to make a generous donation if they'd take in a wayward, headstrong, overbearing, spoiled daughter. But maybe Douglass could use a few well-trained tears on her father. Perhaps she could convince Michael Sullivan to override her mother's hot Mexican blood and send her off to Ireland for a year. She'd hate being away from the ranch and her family that long, but anything would beat the convent or another grueling day like the one she'd just had. Honestly, she was more than ready to go home; ready to go ahead and face the music. Tell them all that she'd been stupid, even if it did hurt her pride just thinking about it.

The maid took the small table and the dirty dishes with her when she left and Douglass commenced to shedding her filthy clothing. She eased down into the hot water with a sigh which came all the way from the bottom of her soul. She enjoyed the water until it was stone cold, then with another sigh wished she could call for a second bath. But that was just too extravagant and besides Monroe would never let her live down that kind of thing.

She washed her sweaty underthings in the bath water, along with her shirt and trousers, hoping they'd be dry by morning. If not, she'd have to wear them damp since that's all she had. She wondered what Monroe was doing in the room right next to hers. She'd heard the maid opening and shutting the door as she carried pitchers of water in his room also. His boots made a thud when he took them off but, even listening intently, she couldn't tell when he'd slipped into his tub of hot water. Did he enjoy it as much as she had? Or was he such a tough and mean Yankee that even a good hot bath was something he took for granted? Not that it mattered one bit to her how he felt about anything. Tomorrow she would be on the next stage headed south back to DeKalb, Texas. Her grandmother would take sides with her. She wouldn't let them put her in a convent. Douglass could always twist Abulita around her pinkie finger and she'd practice weeping uncontrollably all the way home. Abulita hated tears.

Douglass fell asleep with a smile on her face. Things would be wonderful.

Monroe fought back the inner feeling of trouble on the wind, fearing it had manifested itself in the form of a lady in the next room. Nothing he had to do between Galveston, Texas and Love's Valley, Pennsylvania was life threatening. He had survived the war years and a year in the south of Texas trying to help with the reconstruction. All he had to do now was deliver some papers, report to a few generals on the way, and then go home.

He told himself before he fell asleep that he'd be the happiest man in the world if he woke up tomorrow morning and found an empty room next to his.

You could always put her on a stage and send her back to Texas. You don't have to take her another mile further. You don't owe her one thing, Monroe. I'm thinking you like her company. You like the way she keeps you entertained with her grit and sass, his conscience told him bluntly.

He didn't even argue with the inner voice baiting him into a fight. He just shut his eyes and fell asleep, but he would not awaken the happiest man in the world the next morning.

Douglass awoke with a groan, the sun streaming through the window right into her eyes, when Monroe slung open the door and marched in like he owned the place and didn't like it. He stood there at the end of her bed, staring at her as if she was some kind of prize piece of horse flesh he intended to purchase that day. Disappointment was written all over his handsome fresh-shaven face, and for the life of her, Douglass couldn't imagine why.

"We've got to catch the stage out of here, so you need to get up, go to the store down the street, and buy an outfit suitable for traveling. I've already been there and left a sum of money so purchase whatever you need. One of those suits women wear when they're not riding a horse. We'll be stop-

ping in North Little Rock this afternoon and staying over in
that town. I have a meeting to attend, possibly a dinner. If
there is a dinner, you will attend with me. It will be obvious
when I arrive that we are traveling together. I will tell the
general I'm meeting with that you are a distant relative I am
escorting back to Pennsylvania. You won't spoil it, will you
Douglass?" Monroe asked coldly.

"A Yankee General?" She snarled her nose and peeped at
him through slits, still trying to get her eyes to open fully.

"Yes, a Yankee General." He nodded seriously.

"Well then, darlin', I can sure tell a Yankee general a
bold-faced lie like that. Now if it was a Rebel general, I'd
shoot myself before I lied to him," she answered, just as
coldly. "Now get out of here so I can get my clothes on and
go do your sweet bidding." She'd have a dress alright, a traveling suit at that, but she was going south instead of north.
"And what are we doing with the horses? Will they run along
behind the stage the whole way to Philadelphia?"

"No, as much as I hate to do it, I'm going to sell Stony
right here in Benton, as well as your horse. The man at the
livery will probably give me a fair price for them both and
we won't need them any more. The rest of our trip can be by
stage. You've got two hours to take care of things. You don't
have time to laze around," he reminded her curtly.

"Then get out of my room." She pointed toward the door.
"I'm not throwing off these covers until you are out of here.
You've already ruined my reputation in one place. Just being
in here would ruin it in this hotel too."

Monroe stormed out of the room, a halo of anger encir-
cling his handsome face and a force of wrath pushing him
out the door. *The audacity of that woman!* He'd found her
sitting on the side of the road, for pity's sake, a sitting duck
for whoever wanted to take advantage of her. He'd saved her
hide from a couple of ruffians who would have ruined more
than her reputation, and what did he get for his efforts but
sass and more sass. He'd be almighty glad to hand her over
to her aging aunt in Philadelphia, wash his hands of the

whole affair, and forget he ever thought he had to be a chival-rous knight in shining armor. A smile tickled the corners of his mouth as he stomped down the stairs. She really did keep him on his toes and kept life from being dull, didn't she?

The trousers and shirt were still slightly damp, but Douglass put them on anyway, along with her boots. She braided her hair and wrapped the ropes around the top of her head like a halo so her wide brimmed straw hat would fit. She met Monroe waiting at the foot of the stairs, tapping his foot. Were all Yankees so impatient? If they were, it's a won-der all the women up north didn't migrate to the south where the men were trained from birth to cherish women and to wait for them patiently.

"I'm going to the stage station to make arrangements," he said stiffly. "Like I said before, I've already been to the store and left enough money to cover anything you need."

"I told you," she hissed, dark eyebrows knitting together in the middle in a serious frown, "that I'd buy my own clothes."

"And I told you money isn't the issue here," he whispered gruffly. "Go on and meet me back here, ready to go, in thir-ty minutes."

"I'll sure enough be ready to go and that's a fact," she said, smiling up into his face sweetly.

She'd smiled and it looked genuine and sincere, so why was he doubtful? It could be because she hadn't thanked him for his financial help or it could be that she was getting ready to run away. Well, if she took off she was on her own. She could fight off highway pirates or join them. Monroe wasn't going to ride to her rescue again.

The door to the general store squeaked when she opened it and a young man who reminded her of Raymond looked up from the counter at the back of the store. "Could I help you?" he asked, no warmth in his voice.

"I'm here to purchase a dress," she said.

"Oh." He flushed scarlet. "I'm sorry ma'am. I thought you was a young boy."

"I've been riding," she murmured by way of an excuse.

"Well, I'm sorry to disappoint you ma'am, but we don't have any ready-made dresses in stock," he said. "Would you be the lady that Monroe Hamilton left money in my care for? He said there'd be a lady coming in a few minutes and I was to sell her whatever she needed."

"Yes, I am." She nodded, letting her hat fall back, revealing the braids on top of her head and the clearest blue eyes the young man had ever seen.

"Well, why don't I give you the poke he left with me. There's a dress shop two doors down. Mable usually has a few things made up ready for sale. If you got time to wait, she could make you something in a week," he said, his voice hopeful that the pretty woman would stick around Benton for a while.

"I've got less than two hours." She smiled brightly at him. "Thank you for pointing me in the right direction."

"Sure thing." He sighed, his heart firmly attached to his sleeve.

Mable was pulling back the drapes to the two outside windows when Douglass stepped inside the store. She'd purposely left her hat hanging down her back so that Mable would know she was dealing with a woman and not a teenaged boy. That stuck in Douglass' craw more than she'd like to admit. Knowing her own assets as well as flaws, she didn't see where anyone should take her for a boy, not with her ample bosom and tiny waist. Evidently the loose fitting shirt and trousers covered up an awful lot.

"Help you, madam?" Mable asked.

"Yes, I need a traveling suit and perhaps something fit to attend an important dinner," Douglass replied as she snapped out of her reverie.

"Wouldn't have a thing for a dinner, I'm afraid. Not already made anyway. If you've got a week, I could sew anything you'd like." Mable pulled a deep blue full skirt and matching shirt from a rack. "Made this last week for a lady about your size. She thought she was going east then changed her mind. Said she'd buy it anyway if it didn't sell in a couple of weeks."

"That will do fine," Douglass said. "Would you have a hat to match?"

"Sure would. Made it to match. I'm a milliner too. But the hat is over at the general store in the window. Thought I might have a better chance at selling it there since so many folks go in to buy other things," Mable said.

"Then I'll go back and buy it. Don't suppose you'd have a pair of drawers and a camisole, maybe a corset in my size."

"Keep them all the time. Just white cotton lawn though. Don't have much call for the silk in these parts, especially since everyone is so poor after the war. Where you from, anyway, girl? You got an accent that tells me you aren't from here." Mable wrapped the suit and underthings in brown paper, all the while eyeing the lovely woman before her.

"West Texas. Little town called DeKalb," Douglass told her.

"Where you going?" Mable asked.

"South." Douglass smiled. "Back home."

"Well, I hope you enjoy the suit." Mable handed the package to her. "That will be five dollars for all of it."

Douglass paid the lady. Looking forward to dressing like a woman again and riding in a stage rather than a saddle, she almost hummed as she went back to the general store to buy the matching hat. She didn't care if it cost as much as all the other items together or if it hair-lipped the governor of the great state of Texas, she was going have it. After all, according to the ill-tempered Yankee captain, money wasn't the issue here.

The young man at the counter beamed when she opened the door, and flirted blatantly as he put the hat into a box and handed it to her, purposely letting his fingertips touch hers. Even though she didn't feel a thing for the very young gentleman, it felt good to be admired and desired again, to be treated like a southern lady and playfully flirted with. *Maybe Monroe should stay in the south a while longer and learn some manners,* she thought as she passed a table covered in fabrics, lace, and ribbons. She stopped long enough to finger the satin ribbon, wondering if she should buy a length to entwine in her hair if she was called upon to attend a dinner, then chastised herself for not remembering that she was leaving Monroe's company as soon as she could get out of the pants and shirt and into the feminine traveling suit. Yes sir, Douglass Esmerelda Sullivan was on her way back home, where she had no doubt she could wheedle her way back into the family's good graces within twenty-four hours.

Douglass heard the back door of the store open and shut and the young man begin talking to someone else. Most likely the real proprietor of the store. The boy looked far too young to own the place. The murmur of voices went on for a few minutes, then the door shut again. She fingered the ribbon one more time, the soft satin reminding her of by-gone days before the war came and everything was torn apart; days when she danced all night with pretty ribbons in her hair.

The door squeaked and Douglass looked up from behind the table, expecting to see Monroe storming inside the store and demanding that she stop dawdling and get back to the hotel. If it was, then there was no time like the present to tell him that she'd changed her mind and was going home. She'd hand him the small leather poke with the rest of his money, ask for his address so her parents could reimburse him, and thank him like a true southern lady should. Surely he wouldn't pitch a fit in a public place. Most likely, he'd drop down on his knees and give thanks he was finally getting rid of the baggage that had aggravated him every turn of the way.

"Well, I'll tell you one thing," one of the men said as he shut the door with a bang, "she'd better be ready to spend the rest of her life in prayer and meditation."

Icy shivers skipped down Douglass' spine when she realized who had slammed that door. Her second oldest brother, Colum, and the youngest, Flannon now stood in the store.

She eased her sombrero back onto the top of her head and tiptoed toward the door, but not in time. Flannon stopped not four feet from her with only a tall display of shoes on a rack separating them. She had to fight back the urge to fall into Colum's arms and tell him the whole sordid story, but something kept her still a moment longer.

"This time even tears aren't going to bring Daddy to his knees," Flannon said. "Not after we tell him what that lady of the night said. Momma is going to have a pure Mexican hissy fit when she finds out that Esmie was sharing a bed with a Yankee soldier. I wonder what is going on."

"Raymond threw her out and left her on the side of the road or else she left him. We know that much for sure. We also know that the sorry scoundrel bragged to me the night before we found her note that he had a little Mexican doxy lined up to keep him company on the trip back East. I asked him who it was and if he was going to marry her. He laughed really hard and said he didn't kiss and tell and it would be a cold day in hell when he married her. We know the Mexican doxy was Esmie and that she probably thought she was getting married. What I figure is that the Yankee found her there and she took up with him. Who'd a thought such a thing of Esmie? She could have had any man in northern Texas and she took up with that sorry Raymond. I could shoot Nick for bringing him home."

"Let's just go home. She's got to get tired of this and come on back any day now," Flannon whispered.

"Don't matter now. She's slept with that Yankee and Momma will put her in a place where she won't disgrace the Montoya or Sullivan name again. Hope she likes lots of prayers. Maybe she'll get a room with Cousin Bertha. That's where Momma will put her and you know it," Colum said. "Now let's go ask this fellow if he's seen anyone like her."

Abulita? Douglass thought silently, her knees turning to jelly. Surely her grandmother would take her side and keep her from being sent away.

As if he read her mind, Colum shook his head, slapped his black hat against his thigh, and said, "Even Abulita is so mad she could spit tacks. Know what she told me before we left? She said if her disgraceful granddaughter watered the whole state of Texas during a drought with her tears, she would never forgive her for hurting the family. Said that bad blood must run in the girls in the family. First Cousin Bertha and now Esmie."

Douglass' heart fell to the toes of her boots, turned cold as ice, and broke into thousands of sharp pieces. She wasn't welcome at home again. Not if even Abulita was angry with her. She'd be put away, never to see the ranch or ride a horse again. She'd only see her family when they came to the cold convent to see her, and with their anger so raw, that might not happen for a good many years.

"Hey, have you seen a Mexican lady about this tall?" Colum held his hand out and asked the man behind the counter. Douglass figured her running days were over, sure as shootin'.

"Can't say as I have. But I've only been here a few minutes. Willie, my nephew, opens the store for me in the mornings and keeps it until he has to go to school. He's in his final year down at the high school. Smart boy, going to help me full time when he gets out," the older man said. "He didn't mention anyone like that coming in, though. We don't get many ladies out and about this early, anyway. Sorry I can't help you fellows. Why are you looking for her anyway?"

"She's our sister and we're tracking her down. She's run away from home. But we'll find her and take her home where she belongs. Right after we give her a piece of our minds," Flannon told the man.

"The war has made lots of people do strange things," the man said. "Don't be too rough on her until you find out the truth of the matter."

Thank you, Douglass thought.

"There ain't enough rough in the world to cover what I'm

going to do to her when I get a hold of her," Colum said coldly. "Breaking Momma's heart and putting Daddy through pure hell. She's the only daughter, come after six of us boys, and she's in big trouble. She's somewhere in this town. I can feel it. We found a camp down the road about thirty miles and we've ridden all night."

"Might be they caught the midnight stage going to Little Rock," the man said. "There's one leaves every night at midnight then another sometime in the morning."

"Ain't that our luck," Flannon groaned. "Well, let's get on with it, Colum. We'll stop at the stage station and see if she's bought a ticket. If not we'll go on to Little Rock and see if we can catch her there."

Well, they darn sure haven't ridden off their mad yet, Douglass thought as she opened the door so slowly it didn't even squeak and shut it as carefully. She wasted no time getting back across the street and up the stairs to her room. She watched out the window as her two brothers mounted their horses, rode down the street to the stage station and stayed a few minutes before coming out and riding north out of town. Tears flowed down her cheeks as she wished desperately she could go back and change the last few days. So Raymond had even bragged about her, calling her a Mexican doxy, had he? Well, she'd enjoy putting a long blade through his black heart. As Colum and Flannon rounded a bend in the road and disappeared she wiped away the tears. To hug them both to her and tell them she was sorry wouldn't work. Not right now. Maybe in a few weeks, they'd catch up to her and she'd be able to convince them how sorry she really was.

When Monroe knocked on the door and entered the room without waiting for a reply she was fully dressed in her new suit. Her hat was set at the right angle above the bun at the nape of her neck, and for all the world she looked like a respectable young lady on her way to visit an aging aunt in the East. Not even Monroe noticed the redness around her eyes.

His heart skipped a beat when she turned from the window. If circumstances had been different he might have had the notion to court Douglass Sullivan. But they weren't, and it was probably for the better. He'd sworn that he'd be a bachelor the rest of his life, and not even a lovely lady like the one before him could break through his war-hardened heart.

"I see you are ready," he said, grouchiness icing every word to cover the fact that his mouth was dry and his mind reeling.

"Yes, I am, and thank you for the gift of all these lovely things," she said sweetly. "My aunt will reimburse you for all your expenses if you will but keep a tab. After all, my own things had to be left, and I do appreciate your care and concern."

His heart flipped around in his chest like a teenager with a crush on the schoolteacher who'd said he did well on the spelling test. His mind went into overtime trying to figure out what had happened from the time he had left her until now while the antsy feeling that did not usually steer him wrong wrung his insides into knots.

"You are welcome," he mumbled. "The stage leaves half an hour earlier than the desk clerk thought so we'd better get going. Did you buy a dinner dress?"

"No, there wasn't one available. Here is your poke with the remainder of your money, Captain Hamilton." She handed him the leather bag but was very careful not to touch his fingertips. "And pray tell, would you know the difference between Little Rock and North Little Rock? And how far apart are they and how big are those places?"

Chapter Six

"We will need to get our stories straight," Monroe said, running a finger around the tight-fitting collar. He'd had to rely on ready-made clothing for the dinner party tonight at General Adams' house, and nothing short of custom-made shirts ever fit his broad shoulders and thick neck just right.

"I suppose so." Douglass slipped a few more pins in her thick black hair in an attempt to hold the chaste bun in place. "I'm your cousin, then?"

"Actually, no. You are my cousin by marriage so to speak. Your aunt from northern Texas married my aunt's husband's uncle from Philadelphia. It's a tangled web but we are related by marriage. That way even though we aren't blood kin and since we are related I can escort you without a social black eye," he said, trying hard not to admire the way her dinner gown hugged her shoulders and showed the slightest swell of an ample bosom above the lace ruffling. She'd chosen a dress in a pale blue the same color as her eyes and trimmed in the lightest ecru lace when they'd shopped in a fancy ready-made store late that evening. The hat she picked up and set at a saucy angle like a crown was only the slightest excuse for a hat; merely something to hold the illusive netting bow above the chignon at the nape of her neck.

"Okay, then. It goes like this: Your aunt married this man whose uncle married my aunt. That makes us shirt tail cousins and it's totally acceptable for you to be escorting me

67

to see my relatives," she said. "Now tell me about this General Adams."

Monroe offered her his arm and the two of them stepped out into the hallway of the best hotel in North Little Rock. In its pre-war days, before the invasion, it had been regal, and even now it stood tall and proud. The carpets were a bit shabby from Yankees trudging about without wiping their feet and the furniture was in need of paint and repair, but still holding its head high and proud. Douglass did the same. She held her head up, even though her arm was looped through that of a Yankee officer who she would have gladly strangled and thrown into a ditch for the coyotes to eat, beheaded with a machete, or even clubbed to death with an iron skillet only months before. A woman had to do what a woman had to do to keep herself out of a convent, though, and if attending a dinner party with Monroe Hamilton bought her some time, then she'd bite the bullet and go with him. Truth be known, she was more than a little proud to have her arm looped through that of a man as handsome as the Captain.

"General Adams was a gem in the Union Army. He's been stationed at North Little Rock to oversee the reconstruction. Last August the ex-Confederates swept control of the legislature and passed laws denying black people the right to sit on juries, vote, go to school with white people's children, or even serve in the military. General Adams is working with several other responsible people on a Reconstruction Act that will void the governments of Arkansas plus about eight or nine other states. He's an intelligent, hard-core Army man who is fighting for the betterment of all mankind," Monroe said authoritatively to cover up the tingle in his arm where her gloved hand rested.

Douglass gritted her teeth. How dare these Yankees bring their attitudes and power to the South. They'd already won the war, already completely demolished the old Southern ways. Now they weren't even going to let the Southern people have their own governments back. The world would never be the same. "And I suppose you think that is the way things should be?" she asked.

"Of course. We've fought a war. It's over. Now it's time to rebuild, not only the land and the buildings but the people. The black people have been freed. They have rights like everyone else now," Monroe answered.

"We didn't have slaves. Poppa wouldn't hear of it," she said. "I don't think one person should have the right to own another person, but how on earth can you tell those people who've been slaves that they are now free? Go on out there in the big world where you don't know how to survive without a master and make a living? Don't you think we should be spending some money on helping them learn how to live without a master somehow?"

"It's going to take a long time to get this all on the right track." Monroe's tone was one that he'd have used on Indigo when she was a small child. "Ladies shouldn't worry their pretty heads over politics."

"Of course not," she snapped. "*Ladies* aren't free yet. We're still slaves to the whims, wishes, and wants of men. Someday we'll have to fight a war too, so we can vote and serve in the militia."

Monroe's mouth turned up in half a grin. "The day a woman serves in the militia or votes won't ever dawn, Miss Douglass Sullivan. There's enough men on the face of the earth to keep that from happening without fighting a single battle. Now, I'd ask that you keep your mouth closed on topics of political nature tonight."

"Ask all you want, Captain Hamilton. Sometimes when you ask, the answer is yes, sometimes it's no," she smarted off.

"Well, it had best be yes tonight. I've important business to take care of and if you want an escort to Philadelphia you'd do well to keep your Southern as well as your women's rights opinions locked up in that pretty head of yours. I don't intend to be embarrassed by you," he said as they left the hotel lobby and got into the buggy with General Adams' crest on the side.

"Are you blackmailing me?" she asked, arranging the full skirt of her dress on the buggy seat in an attempt to keep the wrinkles at bay. "Because if you are, I'm perfectly capable of going to Philadelphia by myself from this point. I've got money and I'm able to make arrangements at stage stations, I'm quite sure."

It was his turn to grit his teeth. She was a handful, this Mexican-Irish beauty from Texas, and if he had a lick of sense he'd tell the driver to take her to the nearest station himself. "Just keep your political views to yourself at dinner. That's an order, not a request, so there isn't an option of saying yes or no."

"There's always an alternative," Douglass whispered loud enough that he had to strain to hear the words.

Douglass and Monroe were met in the foyer of a magnificent old Southern home on the outskirts of North Little Rock by General Adams and his lovely wife Geraldine. Silver streaks laced the general's dark brown hair and he towered over Monroe, long and lanky with a gleam in his eyes when he shook the Captain's hand. Only friends of long-standing would be so comfortable in each other's presence, Douglass thought as she was introduced to the general and then to his wife. Geraldine was at least twenty years his junior. Her blond hair was piled high on her head and she was a tall woman, but she did little more than come up to the general's shoulder. Questions riddled her green eyes and for a fleeting moment Douglass had the impression she'd seen Geraldine before.

Douglass smiled demurely during the introductions, then deepened her pure Texas drawl into a smooth southern tone that caused Geraldine's eyebrows to raise almost to the second story ceiling where a crystal chandelier sparkled with candle lights.

"Oh, my dear, you are from the South." Geraldine caught her breath.

"Yes, ma'am. Texas, to be more exact." Douglass nodded ever so slightly.

"Lovely accent," General Adams commented graciously, then ignored her completely. "Did you bring the papers? I have a full report to send with you to Washington. We'll retire to the parlor after dinner," he told Monroe, who nodded agreeably.

Dinner was in the formal dining room. Candles in silver holders were strewn down the middle of a table meant to seat a dozen people. Fresh cut fall flowers—asters, mums, marigolds, even a few fall roses—were arranged in sparkling crystal vases. The General sat at one end of the long table with his wife to his right, Douglass beside her, and Monroe on his left.

"How beautiful," Douglass sighed when Monroe seated her in the velvet-padded chair. Where on earth had they found such luxuries in a war torn country?

"Yes, we do try to keep up appearances. It's actually a help to the reconstruction, you know," Geraldine said graciously.

Dinner, a six course repast, lasted two hours, and the conversation flitted from the salary of a good cook to how much longer it would be before the first frost, killing off the roses and fresh flowers. Geraldine declared that she really should put in a small green house so she could grow flowers all year round. After all, flowers really did dignify a party, didn't they?

Douglass slowly and carefully ate cream of potato soup sprinkled with fresh parsley and avoided voicing her opinions. If they wanted to converse about such mundane things they were wasting precious time. She wondered briefly if this was the way all Yankees ate their evening meals—seated around a huge table, paid servants bringing them their food and clearing away the china between courses. Was that so very different from the Southern ways before the war? Yes, she told herself, it was. Because the servants toting and bringing were being paid to do so and were doing it of their own volition, not because they were slaves and would be punished if they didn't.

"So Douglass, where in Texas are you from?" Geraldine asked.

"Little place up north called DeKalb," Douglass answered, wiping her mouth daintily with the crisp, ironed linen napkin. For some reason she couldn't see Geraldine sweating over a flat iron doing up napkins.

"DeKalb?" General Adams was suddenly interested.

Monroe's head snapped up and he forgot all about the soup he'd been enjoying. So did the good general know something of that area? Would he be able to tell Monroe later that evening anything about Douglass' people? Monroe certainly hoped so.

"Yes, are you familiar with DeKalb?" Douglass asked, hoping the man was just showing a gentlemanly interest.

"Of course, I am. Geraldine and I took a couple of weeks at the beginning of summer and went down there. We bought two brood mares and had them delivered. There's a family there that grows the best horses in the country. Well known for their training. Geraldine and I both love horses and have decided to raise them ourselves. We have bought a big ranch north of here and we're staying in Arkansas. I may run for a government office if all goes as planned. Geraldine says she's had enough of the Northern winters to last her a life-time. I understand Michael Sullivan's in-laws, the Montoyas, started that business a long time ago," General Adams said. "So are you of that Sullivan family. I never put the two together until right now."

Monroe cut his eyes across the table, dark eyebrows knitting together in the middle of his lined forehead. She really had lied to him about being an orphan. He hoped she was sweating bullets.

"Yes, I am. Michael is my father. The Montoyas are my grandparents," Douglass said, looking across the table into Monroe's furious eyes. So now he knew. What could he do about it? It didn't mean that she wasn't still going to Philadelphia to spit in Raymond's eye.

"But they didn't call you Douglass. Is that really your name?"

"Yes it is. Momma is Mexican and she named all of us the middle name, and Daddy is Irish and he named the first name. By the time I was born, he'd given up on ever having a daughter so he'd chosen the name Douglass. When I surprised everyone, he didn't change the name," she explained.

"But they called you Esmie or something like that," Geraldine said.

Douglass cut her eyes across the table to find the frown disappearing from Monroe's face as he fought back a chuckle. Damn his black heart anyway. Now he knew her middle name and she didn't know his.

"It's short for Esmerelda," she said coldly, not blinking. He could rot in hell if he teased her or started calling her either Esmerelda or Esmie.

"I see, and it's one of your aunts who lives in Philadelphia?" Geraldine asked. "I knew you looked familiar when Monroe introduced you to us. You are the exact image of your mother, a very lovely and gracious woman. All except those eyes. They came straight from Michael, your father."

"Yes, of course, I'm going to Philadelphia to stay with my aunt for a while." Douglass replied, not backing down a bit from all the questions locked up behind Monroe's dancing black eyes.

"Does your aunt live right in Philly?" Geraldine asked.

"Oh no, she and my uncle have a huge farm outside of town. You probably wouldn't know them." Douglass shifted her eyes away from Monroe who positively had smoke spewing from his ears and out the top of his head.

"With milk cows? I was raised up in that area. We used to get milk from John Wilson every morning. It wouldn't be John and Hilda, would it?" Geraldine squeezed Douglass' leg under the table.

"Of course it is. Small world indeed, isn't it?" Douglass said, wondering why in the world this woman was helping her out of an impossible situation.

"Oh my, yes," Geraldine smiled. "Strange how we keep meeting people who know people we know."

"I never met a John and Hilda Wilson," the general said flatly.

"Naturally not," Geraldine said sweetly. "Hilda's oldest daughter Chloe, was my good friend when we were in school. John and Hilda had about seven or eight children and raised them on the farm. They'd all be grown by now, I'm sure."

Douglass busied herself with the main course and tried desperately to keep all the names Geraldine was throwing out securely in her mind. "I'm sure they are," she said. "Uncle John died, you know. Broke his heart that he couldn't fight in the war. At least that's what Aunt Hilda wrote to Momma. One day she found him out at the barn with his cows. He'd fallen in a mound of hay and was already cold by the time she got to him. She and the boys run the farm now but Chloe has moved to New York City. Aunt Hilda can use some feminine company and I can use a few months away from Texas," she said, keeping the fabrication going.

"I'm so sorry," Geraldine said. "Well, it certainly is a small world, isn't it? Now, let's have dessert and then these gentlemen can take their coffee and cigars to the parlor and talk politics while we go to the sitting room and have a bit of woman talk," Geraldine suggested.

Even with the amusement in his eyes, Monroe's glare left no doubt that she'd have some explaining to do before either of them got a moment's rest that night. Pure ice flowed from his usually warm fingertips when his hands brushed her shoulders as he led her to the sitting room. The scowl on his face when he excused himself with the general would have melted a less sassy woman. Douglass almost looked forward to the encounter; she'd been the serene little Southern belle all day, ever since she'd had that close call with her brothers in the general store in Benton. Douglass could only stand playing such a dignified role for so long. It was past time for a rousting good argument. One which she surely intended to win.

"So what's really going on?" Geraldine's face split into a grin followed by a rich giggle making her bosom jiggle.

"Why, nothing, Miz General Adams," Douglass drew out each word in exaggerated Texas accent. "Whatever are you talking about?"

"There is no Aunt Hilda or Uncle John," Geraldine said. "You're caught."

"I figured as much and I'm beholden to you for the help. Lord, Monroe is going to be an old bear with an ingrown toenail as it is. If you hadn't helped me, he would have shot flames all the way to Philadelphia," Douglass said.

"You are welcome. It was fun. Now tell me what's going on." Geraldine patted the settee.

Douglass fanned her skirts out as she sat down beside the lady, not sure she wanted to divulge the whole sordid tale to a stranger. She hesitated just long enough that Geraldine grew impatient.

"How in the world did a rich Southern horse rancher's daughter become tangled up with Monroe Hamilton, the heartthrob of every woman in this half of the country?" Geraldine asked.

Douglass figured she owed the woman something since she'd so gallantly rescued her at the dinner table, so she explained, telling the truth about the whole matter, up to and including how that Raymond had literally played her for a fool of the greatest proportions. Geraldine sighed at times and patted Douglass on the shoulder at others.

"I know Raymond Pierce very well. We're both from Philadelphia and our parents had the same circle of friends. He has always been a spoiled brat. He has a horrible reputation in Philadelphia. You were wise to do what you did, Douglass. Is that really your name?" Geraldine said.

"You know Raymond?" Douglass asked incredulously. "And yes, it really is my name." It was indeed a small world in reality as much as in the imaginary world she had created.

"Sure I know him, and why do you go by Douglass now? I swear they called you Esmie."

"Yes they did call me Esmie, but I'm Douglass from now on. Everytime someone says Esmie I think of the sneer on Raymond's face when he told me he'd beat me if I didn't go to bed with him. I never liked the name anyway. My grandmother just hated the idea of me having a boy's name so she refused to call me Douglass. Now I remember you and the general," she said, changing the subject. "Abulita—that's my grandmother—and I had gone into town for the day to look at a new shipment of fabric. We passed you at the gate. You were leaving as we were coming back home that day," Douglass said.

"That's right. I remember too. You and your grandmother waved as our buggies passed each other," Geraldine said. "I caught a fleeting glimpse of you and mentioned to the general how much you looked like your mother. Now, what do you intend to do once you get to Philly? I mean there is no Aunt Hilda or Cousin Chloe. What do you intend to tell Monroe then?" Geraldine asked.

"I expect my brothers, Colum and Flannon, will find me long before that time. If they don't, I'm going to march into the newspaper and spit in Raymond's eye, then I suppose I'll get on the next stage coming back to Texas," she replied.

"I bet you will too," Geraldine said. "But what makes you think those brothers will catch up to you. They wouldn't have to if you worked at it a little bit, and I'd love to see Raymond Pierce embarrassed. I bet I've got a couple of ideas to help you."

"Colum has always been the best Sullivan for tracking. He could track a bumble bee in a snow storm and catch him before nightfall. Besides, I saw them this morning and they're still pretty angry with me. Overheard them talking about sending me to a convent since I've disgraced the

Montoya and Sullivan names. They know I'm traveling with a Yankee and that I slept with him. And they're only a few hours away from finding me," Douglass said.

"You've slept with Monroe? Lord, girl, there's a string of women from the East Coast to the Gulf of Mexico who'd like to have that privilege. How'd you manage that?" Geraldine said.

"We slept. Really—shut your eyes, go to sleep, wake up, nothing more," Douglass' cheeks turned scarlet.

"I've got to hear this story too. Hurry, they won't take forever in there with their politics. Monroe is delivering some papers and taking some along with him. They're using him as a courier since he's on his way home anyway," Geraldine said. "Now talk."

Douglass told her more of the story, beginning with how she stole the horse and ending with the night they spent in a brothel.

"I can't wait until next week. It's my turn to have tea on Thursday afternoon. This is a delightful tale to tell the women." Geraldine all but clapped her hands.

"You wouldn't dare!" Douglass exclaimed.

"I will," Geraldine nodded. "Monroe, with all his ellusive, standoffish, egotistical ways deserves it. You'll be down the road past Memphis by then so you'll never suffer the repercussions of it. Besides it's my reward for the trick we're going to pull on your brothers and Monroe tomorrow morning."

Douglass smiled. Like the woman said, she'd be long gone.

"You said you had some ideas? Why would you help me?" Douglass asked.

"Because Raymond needs a woman to dress him down and you're just the one to do it," Geraldine replied. "Now let's put our heads together and figure this out. And if everything fails and he sends you back to Texas, you get off in Benton and send me a telegraph. I'll either come get you or send someone trustworthy. After all, your cousin was my best friend when we were growing up in Pennsylvania. I couldn't let you go to a convent. You'd simply have to live here with me until we could find you a proper husband." Geraldine laughed.

"I don't want a husband. After that business with Raymond, I may decide to be an old maid," Douglass said with a heavy sigh.

"Oh, no you won't. Not someone as lovely as you." Geraldine giggled.

"Thank you," Douglass said. She could scarcely believe that a Yankee woman had made so generous an offer. She couldn't see herself living in a Yankee household, especially one that was determined to undermine the Arkansas government as it stood, but, then again, it wasn't as difficult to envision as the scene where she stayed on her knees half the day praying for the sins of her wayward heart.

"Okay, the truth and nothing but the truth," Monroe demanded as he folded his arms over his broad chest.

"I'm not an orphan, but I was on my way to Philadelphia for real. Only thing is that I thought I was eloping with Raymond and it turned out he wanted a bed partner for the trip. The rest of the story is the truth except I'm not an orphan. I can't go back. My mother would be scandalized if she knew everything that has happened and they'd for sure put me in a convent," she said flatly. "It's been a long evening and I didn't one time scream out my political views or crawl up on a soap box about women's rights. Could I go to sleep now?"

An uneasy feeling tightened around his heart. She was telling the truth but not all of it, he'd almost swear. Geraldine, who he'd trust with his very life, had known her Aunt Hilda and Uncle John so that part must be true. Yet, if it was, what part was a fabrication or an exaggeration?

"Well?" Douglass pointed toward the door, standing slightly ajar. As if that would matter anyway. She'd already been caught in bed with the man in a brothel and two of her brothers knew it. Most likely her whole family now also knew it, because as meticulous as Colum was, he'd be sending home telegrams regularly.

"No, we have something to do first," Monroe said, his eyes barely more than slits as he glared down at her. "Does your aunt even know you are coming?"

"No, she doesn't," Douglass said shortly. "I told you the truth. Raymond enticed me to run away with him and I was fool enough to think he meant marriage. I'd figured I would see Aunt Hilda and tell her about the marriage. When I insisted I be left beside the road, I made up my mind to go on to Philadelphia because Daddy and Momma would be so angry with me."

"Then you shall go east," Monroe said. "Only you are going to write your folks a letter and also one to your aunt. That's the only way I'm going to continue to escort you. If you aren't willing to let your parents know you are alive and well and going to stay with your aunt until this all blows over, then you can get on the next stage south and go home tomorrow. I'm not going to survive the war just to hang from the gallows for kidnapping a Southern woman. Writing two letters and mailing them will give me the respectability of being considered an escort."

Her mouth set itself in a firm line and her lightly-toasted skin turned brilliant red. How dare him lay down an ultimatum like that to her. "I'm not writing letters," she smarted off, removing her hat and setting it carefully on the dresser.

"Then goodnight, Douglass Sullivan. I will take you to the stage tomorrow morning and send you home to face your convent," he said stoically as he slung open the door.

"Okay, okay!" She stomped her foot hard enough to rattle the pitcher and washbowl on the wash stand. "I'll write the letters."

"Good," he nodded seriously. "I'll leave you to them then. And we will mail them on our way out of town at first dawn.

The post office and stage station are one and the same so it will be easy for you to do."

"Yes, sir." She saluted mockingly.

"Give me your word that you'll be truthful in both letters and I won't even read over your shoulder," he said.

"You've got my word that I won't tell a single lie in the letters," she said.

He didn't answer as he shut the door gently. She longed to jerk it open and slam it hard enough to wake everyone on the whole second floor of the hotel. Or double up her fist and dot his eye for his almighty powerful insolence. Thank goodness Geraldine was willing to help her out with her brothers or she'd be in a convent next week for sure. But how was she supposed to write one letter, much less two, with no paper?

As if Monroe had read her mind through the wall separating their rooms, he appeared at her door with two sheets of paper, two envelopes, a quill pen and a bottle of ink. He set them on the dresser without a word and was out of the room before she could think of a single smart remark to burn his ears with.

She shot the bolt home to lock the door. Drat his sorry soul anyway, acting like he was the parent and she was nothing more than an errant child. At least he'd have to knock before he entered her private room again. She threw her shawl over the back of the rocking chair and sat down on the vanity bench in front of the dresser. The sigh came out more like the snort from an overheated horse, but she picked up the bottle of ink and opened it, careful to keep it to the back of the dresser. Spilling ink on her dinner gown would surely bring on the tears of frustration currently hiding behind the thick black lashes. Douglass was determined not to shed a single tear again. She'd be drawn and quartered if one sorry old Yankee and two pieces of paper would bring on tears.

Dear Daddy and Momma, she wrote and then stared at the ceiling, batting her eyelashes to keep back the river floating around her clear blue eyes. One piece of paper for each meant she had to get the message right the first time. *I am fine.* He said she had to tell them what she was doing and where she was going so they wouldn't worry. Well, she'd told them she was fine, wasn't that enough? Probably not. She dipped the pen again and began to write. *Momma, you've always said that when a woman has something laid upon her heart she has to do it. Well, I have to take care of something and then I will come home. Sometimes things are not what they appear to be, and this is one of those times. Please trust me. I'll be home and tell you the whole story in a few weeks. Your daughter who loves you both, Douglass Esmerelda Sullivan*

The letter to her fictitious Aunt Hilda was much easier to write. She told the Aunt that she'd be arriving in Philadelphia in a few weeks. That wasn't a lie. Then she went on to fill the front of the sheet of plain white stationary Monroe had given her. Blowing on the ink gently to dry it, she thought of several other things she could say, so she turned the paper over and wrote another half a page about her father and her brothers. None of it lies.

Leaving the letter to dry on the dresser, she removed her dinner gown, folded it gently, and laid it in the small trunk Monroe had insisted she purchase that afternoon when they'd arrived in North Little Rock. She'd need the dress several times as they stopped across the country on their way to Washington D.C. Besides, a lady didn't travel without a trunk, and she had to pretend to be a lady.

"Pretend?" She muttered to herself before she went to sleep. "I am a lady. One on the run right now, but I am a lady. If I'd been anything less I would be traveling with the dishonorable Raymond Pierce rather than the honorable Captain Hamilton."

That brought her comfort as she shut her eyes. But it was short-lived because she proceeded to dream about Monroe Hamilton in a Union uniform, his black eyes and handsome face mocking her. She awoke at daylight in a cold sweat, wondering if she wouldn't be wise to get on that stage for Benton and wire Geraldine to come and get her. She hurriedly dressed in her traveling suit and was putting on her hat when Monroe knocked at the door.

"Letters?" he asked, without even so much as a polite good morning.

She nodded toward the dresser where one still lay drying, the other in the envelope and properly addressed.

"Good," he said, picking up the letter to her folks and holding it up to the sunshine flowing into the room through lace curtains. Through the envelope he could see writing so she had kept her word. "I will fold this and get it ready to go. What is the address you need on your aunt's letter?"

"Hilda Wilson. Philadelphia, Pennsylvania. She picks up her mail at the post office there like we do in DeKalb," Douglass said in a chilly tone that she hoped froze him to death.

In a flowing script, Monroe addressed the letter and sealed it. "We'll have to hurry a bit. I bought the stage tickets yesterday when we arrived. I've already ordered a basket made from the kitchen containing our three meals today. We will ride until well past dark and sleep in a small hotel in Brinkley," he said, pocketing both letters. One way to be sure they were mailed was to do it himself. Even though she'd given her word, that uneasy feeling surrounded him again, and he wasn't taking any chances. He could be hung for kidnapping a woman, and he had his doubts if Douglass Sullivan would really be honest if it meant his life or her freedom.

They were almost to the station when Geraldine hailed them from a buggy. Douglass covered a smile with the back of a gloved hand. At least this much was going on schedule. She and Geraldine had planned the night before that she would distract Monroe with some kind of tale while Douglass bought a ticket in the opposite direction to throw her brothers off the trail and to buy her a few more days.

Raymond Pierce must have been a rogue of the purest

kind for Geraldine to despise him so much. Douglass was
hoping to have heard some of the stories before the men-
folks came back from the study; now she'd never know. But
she hardly needed fuel to fire her own dislike for the man.
He'd already proven himself to be a rascal. She was just glad
not all Yankees were so despicable. There were good ones in
the world. Take Monroe Hamilton for instance. Willing to
escort her all the way to Philadelphia without expecting
immorality. She blushed as she thought of such a thing.

"Monroe," Geraldine called out. "Good morning,
Douglass, but I really need to speak to Monroe privately."

"Go ahead," Monroe said. "I will meet you at the station.
And in case we're in a big hurry, why don't you mail these. But
remember," he whispered, handing her the letters, "I'm going
to watch you from right here and you'd better hand them to the
man through the window. Don't you try anything silly."

"Wouldn't think of it," Douglass said.

The man behind the ticket window grinned from one ear
to the other when Douglass walked up. "Good morning,
ma'am," he said with a flirtatious wink. "And what can I do
for you this morning?"

"I am Douglass Esmerelda Sullivan and I would like to
purchase a ticket to Conway, Arkansas, and I need to mail
this letter," she said deftly putting the letter to Hilda Wilson
on the shelf and pocketing the other inside the folds of her
sweeping dark navy blue skirt.

"We don't care what your name is ma'am, so long as
you've got the money to pay for the ticket and the postage.
Stage for Conway leaves at nine o'clock. You going to wait
here?" he asked, producing the postage for the letter.

She dug in her reticule and brought out enough money to
take care of the ticket as well as the letter. "No, I'm booked
at the hotel down the street. I'll be staying there until just a
few minutes before the stage leaves. Why are you asking?"

"Well, I have a short break in a few minutes. Thought I
might buy you some breakfast," the man said. "Why are you
going to Conway?"

"Thank you, but no. I'm running away from two brothers who've been sent to bring me back home. Please don't tell them I was here," she pleaded with the ticket taker. So that's how unescorted women were treated, she thought. They were winked at, asked to go to breakfast with perfect strangers, became doxies. She'd have a devil of a time just getting back to DeKalb all on her own. A cold chill embraced her heart. She did need Monroe, whether she wanted to admit it or not.

"Wouldn't think of it," he said with another broad wink. "What do these brothers look like?"

"Why, just like me. Half Irish and half Mexican. Only a good bit taller than I am," she said. "I'm going to Conway to marry an old sweetheart but he's a Yankee sympathizer and my brothers are pure Rebel."

"Well, your secret is safe with me," he said.

"Did you get the job done?" Monroe said so close that the warmth of his breath tickled her neck.

"Yes, of course," she said, glad the man had turned away from the window to write down a telegraph message. As Monroe helped her into the east-bound stage, she fingered the letter addressed to her parents deep inside the pocket of her skirt. She held back a soft giggle wondering if there really was a Hilda Wilson in Philadelphia and what she would make of her letter should she ever receive it.

At noon the two Sullivan brothers stopped by the ticket office to ask a few questions. A five-dollar gold piece bought them the information that their sister had indeed bought a ticket for Conway, Arkansas on the 9:00 stage. The ticket man was a pure Rebel himself and he sure wouldn't want his sister marrying up with a Yankee sympathizer. He told the brothers that if they rode fast they most likely could prevent the wedding. Conway was, after all, only a hard day's ride from North Little Rock.

Chapter Seven

Monroe and Douglass rode in silence after they'd exchanged the barest of pleasantries during breakfast. *Here's a biscuit. Would you like a sip of tea from your jar? Have you had enough to sustain you until lunch?* Most of the questions were answered with one word, yes or no. Other than that, no comments were expected or received. They hadn't contracted out to be friends, just traveling companions.

At Lonoke the stage stopped for a brief five minutes to load more passengers. Douglass used the minutes wisely to make a hurried trip to the outhouse behind the station, and was careful to make sure the hostler didn't see her going or coming. If her brothers didn't get the message that she'd gone in the opposite direction, she would need to be very careful about being seen. In a couple of weeks, she was going to step out in public right in front of their noses and let them rescue her. By then they'd be so saddle sore and ready to go back to Texas that they'd forgive her. It would take at least two more weeks to get back home. She'd be sincerely good and docile on the trip back, and by that time, with their good report and the time lapse, Douglass would be back in the good graces of her family—hopefully.

A tall, burly man with a paunchy stomach pushing against the buttons on his vest, along with his wife, a portly woman that matched him perfectly, and their four children, were boarding the stage when Douglass crawled back inside.

There would be no more room for her to fan her skirt tails out with that many passengers. Monroe opened the door, took a look at the crowded seats and slid in next to Douglass.

The father of the family looked in, grunted, and motioned for his oldest son with a crook of the finger. "Okay, Will, you better come on back out of there. Me and you will keep the driver and the shotgun rider company. Ain't no way I'm going to ride with two kids on my lap and that's what it would take. How 'bout you? You want to sit on top?" he asked Monroe.

"No, I think I'll stay here," Monroe said, although sitting on top with the broiling sun pounding down on his black hair might be better than keeping company with a woman who looked like she'd been weaned on a sour pickle, three rambunctious kids, and Douglass.

"Okay. Guess if'n I was still on my honeymoon, I'd think I'd best stay with the new bride too." The man guffawed and slammed the door shut before either Douglass or Monroe could deny the accusation.

She blushed and looked at the ceiling.

He cleared his throat and looked out the window.

"James, you sit there beside the lady. Bertha, you sit beside James. Mandy, you come on over here with me. We'll put the food baskets on the other side of you. You folks can use my seat for your basket too, since you won't have room for it with two kids beside you." The woman organized the whole inside of the coach like an army general. "My name is Clair. Who are you?" she asked bluntly when the coach began to move again.

"I'm Douglass."

"And I'm Monroe Hamilton."

"Right pleased to meet you both. Been traveling long?"

"We're traveling from Texas to Pennsylvania," Monroe said. He could tell the woman that they weren't a married couple, but Douglass' face was still scarlet and he rather liked the feeling of her being put in her place for once.

"Douglass ain't a lady's name," Mandy declared. "It's a boy's name. Why'd your Momma name you Douglass?"

"Mandy, mind your manners." Clair's voice carried little conviction because she also wondered why on earth anyone would call a girl such a name.

"My daddy named me. I've got six brothers and they've all got an Irish first name and a Mexican second name. Momma is Mexican, so she names the middle names. They thought I was going to be another boy and Daddy liked the name Douglass. When I was born a girl, he was so stunned he left the name the same," Douglass explained for what seemed like the hundredth time since she'd left DeKalb.

Clair breathed a sigh of relief. So the woman was half Irish and half Mexican, not a lot better than what Clair figured when she first crawled inside the coach, but still on the edge of being respectable. She hoped the Hamiltons stayed put when she and the children got out in Hazen. That woman looked like she was an octoroon for sure. Clair wouldn't be caught dead riding in the same coach as a woman of color.

"Then you are Yankees?" James asked, in a tone that would have sent a blue norther to freeze the tip of Lucifer's tail right off.

"He is. I am a Texan," Douglass said.

"I don't like Yankees," James said.

"James Fitzpatrick!" His mother slapped him on the knee. "You don't be disrespectful to adults."

"I'm not, Momma. And you know I don't like Yankees. They stole my best friend from me," James pouted, crossing his arms across his narrow chest and sticking his lower lip out as he fought back tears.

"We had two slaves," Clair said. "A cook and her husband who did all the odd jobs around the place. Didn't have a big farm, only a few acres and we didn't really have to have slaves, but we did. They had a couple of little boys, played with my boys, Will and James. 'Course they weren't their best friends, just kids around the place, you know. When they were freed, we didn't have the money to pay them to stay and work so they went on over to Little Rock to get jobs. She's cooking in a big fancy house over there and he's helping with the rebuilding."

"Well, I don't like Rebels," Mandy piped up. "If they hadn't got so fired up and quit the union then we wouldn't have had a war anyway. So it's not all the Yankee's fault."

Monroe smiled.

Douglass frowned.

"Both of you stop it. The war is over and we'll not have a split family because of it," Clair admonished both of them. "You've got to ride in close quarters until we get to Hazen so mind your manners." For the life of her she couldn't understand a marriage between a Yankee and a Rebel, though.

"Why did you marry a Yankee?" James asked.

"James!" his mother admonished.

The young boy began to pout again and threw back the curtain to stare outside.

Douglass was glad she didn't have to answer the question. Explaining why she was traveling with Monroe and not married to him would take longer than letting the issue rest. *What would it be like to be married to Monroe?* She wondered, cocking her head to one side to stare at him from the corner of her eye.

Married to a Yankee? Married to Monroe Hamilton? She resisted a shudder and a giggle both. The laws would have to be rewritten to excuse homicide if that ever happened because she'd sure enough murder him within the first week. In the short time they'd been in each other's company, scarcely an hour passed that they weren't arguing about something.

Goodness only knew, he was handsome enough that she'd have looked twice if he'd been attending parties in northern Texas back before the war. With all that dark hair and those glistening black eyes, yes, she would have flirted. No doubt

about it. But the war had come and was now over and
Monroe had fought on one side, her brothers on the other.
She could never fall in love with such a man.

*But you did. You thought you were in love with Raymond
or you wouldn't have eloped with him.* The inner voice she
was fast coming to hate was right there to correct her.

And I learned my lesson, she thought, battling with a fresh
batch of tears. One minute she wanted to do bodily damage
to Raymond Pierce, to outrun her brothers, to stand on her
own two feet and fight the man who'd ruined her reputation;
the next she wanted to sob until her eyes swelled shut and go
home—no matter the consequences.

Monroe leaned hard against the side of the coach, giving
Douglass all the room he could. The jostling touches of her
shoulder against his, her hip pushing into his, the way she
caught herself by throwing out her hand and bracing against
his knee that one time, it made his mouth dry with desire.
But she'd never know that. Not if he died on the spot. No sir!
Give Douglass that kind of power and she'd drive him insane
before they ever got across the state of Tennessee. So much
for declaring that he would be a bachelor for the rest of his
life. Desires he thought he buried during the war were coming back to haunt him. He might consider taking a wife, after
all. But only a true blue Yankee woman who knew her place.
One who'd bear him children and bring a calm serenity to
his life.

By the time they reached Hazen, Douglass knew Clair's
life history along with her husband's and their parents' and
grandparents'. Her husband had come to Arkansas from
Maine so that explained the split in feelings about the north
and south. Douglass' ears hurt from listening to the woman
for hours on end, and she was glad to see them go on their
merry way. No more passengers boarded in Hazen so
Monroe moved to the other seat and pulled back the window
curtain so he could watch the scenery. Douglass slid down to
the far end of her bench and did the same.

"This is as flat as Texas only with more trees," she said aloud, only making a comment, not really expecting an answer.

"Wait until you see Tennessee," Monroe said without looking at her. "Pine trees that reach up to heaven almost, and on the east side there's mountains. We'll travel on gravel roads that are so high, the rivers and settlements down in the valleys will look like toys."

She shivered. "I'm not sure I'll like that. Anything more than six feet up and I get spooked."

"Then you'd better catch a coach back to Texas, Douglass Esmerelda, because to get to Philadelphia, you've got to travel over not only the Tennessee mountains, but those in Virginia and Pennsylvania also," he commented dryly.

"I'll just have to be spooked," she said. "And my name is Douglass, not Esmerelda and not Esmie, and not Douglass Esmerelda. Just plain old Douglass."

"Yes, ma'am." Monroe shifted his hat over his eyes and leaned back to take a nap.

Stars twinkled in a dark velvet sky by the time they reached Brinkley. Every bone in Douglass ached. The road from North Little Rock to Brinkley had nine million holes in it and the stage driver had managed to hit every one of them. Dust had filtered inside the windows, settling in the creases of her neck, mixing with sweat to form dirt and the much-hated feeling of grime. She hoped it wasn't too late to purchase a bath at the hotel.

Mercy, I only hope it's a real hotel like where we stayed in North Little Rock, and not another brothel, she thought.

Her wishes were not granted. Although it wasn't a brothel, it wasn't anything like the hotel where she and Monroe had spent the previous night. Little more than a two-story house with a bar set up on the first floor and five rooms on the second, the barkeep informed them he was about to shut up for the night but he did indeed have a room, but only one left. It had two beds in it, though. No, he couldn't get baths up the stairs this late but there was plenty of warm water in the reservoir on the stove back in the kitchen if they wanted to carry a bucketful up so they could have a warm water wash before retiring.

Monroe slung open the door to a small room not much bigger than a two hole outhouse. The man had told the truth when he said it had two beds but there was only a foot separating them. The dresser had been painted sometime before the war, not the one the North had won, but the one back in the mid-seventeen hundreds. A mouse skittered across the floor and into a hole right beside the door.

"Welcome to paradise," Monroe said flatly.

"At least it's a bed and not the stage," Douglass replied in an equally flat tone.

"Maybe the one in Hicks Station will be better. That's where we stay tomorrow night. Then we'll get into Memphis late the next afternoon. From there we'll do some sleeping in the coaches for a couple of nights because I want to be in Jackson as quickly as possible," he said, setting her trunk down with a thud. A set of saddlebags on the top slid off onto the floor and he left them there. "I'll go get that bucket of water. We can at least wash up before we fall into those beds. Hope the sheets are cleaner than the room."

Tremors shook Douglass' hands as she turned back the bed she intended to sleep in, the one farthest from that mouse hole. No bugs. Actually the sheets were clean, even ironed, and the pillowcases embroidered with blue birds. "What do you mean, ride all night in a stage?" she asked before he got out of the room.

"It'll be necessary if we're to make it to Washington on time," he said. "I'll get the water and you can have the first wash-up. I'll wait out in the hall until you are in bed. You can turn your back or watch while I wash. Doesn't make any difference to me," he said, a wicked tired grin on his face.

"Hush!" she snapped, already untying her hat.

True to his word, he stepped out into the hallway while she bathed in warm water from a mismatched, cracked pitcher and bowl set on the dresser. She knocked gently on the door when she was finished, then dove into the bed, pulling the covers up under her chin and facing the wall. However, if she turned her head slightly, she could see his reflection in the mirror. At first, she stiffened her neck and shut her eyes so tight they ached. But curiosity eventually got the best of her, and she barely opened one eye—a slit, nothing more—then slowly inched her head a notch to the left and there he was.

Standing with his suspenders drooping around his hips, a broad expanse of chest bare as he washed it, the jet black hair laying flat with the soap and rinse water, then fluffing up when he towel-dried himself. She'd never seen a man with that much hair on his chest and her fingers longed to reach out and touch it, to see if it was truly as soft as it appeared to be. *Wouldn't it be wonderful,* she thought, *to bury her face in all that fur, to fall asleep in his arms, to listen to the easiness of his sleep-induced breathing.* Warm scarlet filled her cheeks at that vision and she feared the bed covers were going to ignite before she could snap her eyes back shut.

"Good night, Douglass," Monroe said as he slipped between his own clean sheets that smelled like they'd been line-dried only yesterday.

"Hmmmm," she feigned sleep, but it was a long time coming again that night.

The next night they stopped at Hicks Station after a long hard day in the coach. They'd only stopped every three hours for fifteen minutes to rest the horses and give the Hamiltons time to find a bush to take care of necessary things. The hotel in Hicks Station at least had two rooms but they made the one at Brinkley look like a mansion. A tiny bed was shoved into one corner, and a wash bowl and pitcher filled with cold water sat on a chair with the back broken off on the other side of the room. The sheets were patched but clean, and Douglass was so tired she didn't even check the walls for mouse holes.

They arrived in Memphis the next afternoon at a few minutes past 3:00. Monroe declared that he had business to attend to which would take two hours. Douglass could wander around town if she wanted, but she was to be back at the stage office at 5:00. They'd have a quick supper in the hotel lobby beside the depot then board the evening coach for Jackson. He'd told her to walk as much as she could because when they boarded this time, they'd be traveling all the way to Jackson, sixty-five miles away, before they stopped again. If everything went well that would be sometime very late the next evening. If not, it would be very early the next morning. After the past two hotels, she couldn't see how the stage could be much worse. And she'd be willing to lay dollars to cow chips that her brothers wouldn't travel all night long in their search for her, so that would give her an edge there too.

Douglass dusted off her skirt tail with the back of her hand and walked down the rough plank sidewalks on the main street of town. She paused in front of a dress shop and admired a hat, a lovely, frothy concoction with lace and feathers. If she'd been in DeKalb, she would have bought it, but there was no way she could wear something like that in a stage, especially if she had to ride with a bunch of children squeezed up next to her. She went on to the next building, a general store, and remembered she needed another handful of hairpins. She lost a couple every day, even at home. The problem was when she was traveling they weren't retrievable.

"No, no, don't hit me no more with that broom. I'll go. I only wanted to see the pretty dolly up close." A little girl was sobbing and running toward the door at the same time Douglass opened it. She barreled into Douglass, the proprietor of the store right behind the child swatting her every few minutes across the back with a broom.

"What is going on?" Douglass grabbed the child and held her close. "Did this child steal something?"

"No, but she knows her kind ain't to come into my store.

They can buy what they need down on the corner. That dirty old Irishman will sell to them. I won't," the woman huffed, out of breath.

"Why?" Douglass asked.

"Because you and her kind ain't welcome here. We mighta had to give you your freedom but we don't have to do business with you," the woman said, eyeing her carefully.

"What do you mean, my kind?" Douglass asked, her temper beginning to boil.

"Don't you play dumb with me, lady. Just get out of my store." The woman waved the broom as if to hit Douglass with it.

Douglass caught it mid-air and pulled it from the woman's hand. Then she looked down to see the child with her face buried deep in Douglass' skirt tails. She had black, kinky pigtails and her skin was a rich ebony. So that's what had upset the woman. A freed slave had had the audacity to step inside her store.

"You better give me that broom and get out of here before I call the sheriff," the woman demanded. "Thing like that could cause another riot and we killed off forty-six of your kind last May. You wouldn't want you and that kid of yours layin' out there in the middle of the street with bullet holes in you would you?"

Douglass handed back the broom. "I'm not a freed slave," she said testily.

"Oh, sure you aren't. You can't fool me. I know black when I see it. Octoroon, or maybe a quadroon, or I'm missing my bet. And with even that much of that kind of blood, you ain't welcome in my store," the woman pointed toward the open door. "Get out."

"I'm Irish and Mexican," Douglass said.

"You're an octoroon!" The woman slammed the door behind her.

"I'm sorry," the little girl said. "Momma said for me not to go in there, but the dolly in the window was so pretty and I wanted to see it better."

"Olivia!" A woman came running down the street, her blue-checked bonnet flying behind her as she hurried. "What have you done, child?"

"She got into trouble when she went in that store. 'Bout a nasty old woman in there," Douglass said.

"And this woman helped me." Olivia grabbed Douglass' hand.

"I see. Well, thank you, ma'am." The mother picked Olivia up and held her tightly.

"Can she come home with us for some cookies?" Olivia asked.

"I am Varley," the mother said.

Her skin was lighter than Olivia's and her eyes were a deep dark green, the rich color of lichen hidden back in the boulders at the ranch in DeKalb. Freckles sprinkled across her nose and cheeks were the only flaw in her perfect skin. Her nose was long and thin, her mouth ready to smile.

"I'm Douglass Sullivan," Douglass introduced herself.

"Would you like to join us for our afternoon cookies?" Varley asked. "We don't live too far. You an octoroon?"

"No, I'm Irish and Mexican," Douglass said again.

"Well, in Memphis, Tennessee, that'd be almost as bad," Varley laughed. "I'm what they call a mulatto. That's where I got these green eyes and freckles, but honey it don't matter. Some of these folks could smell a drop of colored blood and they'd refuse service to you for even that much."

"Evidently." Douglass laughed with her. "And I'd love to come home with you for cookies. I have to be back at the stage depot at five o'clock, though. We'll have to watch the time."

"Ohhhh," Olivia sighed. "Momma, ain't she pretty?"

"Yes, of course, she is," Varley's face lit up in a smile. "And she saved you from a worse whoopin' than what you got. Now let's take her home and thank her proper."

The house Varley led Douglass to was at the end of a street lined with small, unpainted houses. Mums, asters and the last of the fall roses were in full bloom around the porch and Douglass sniffed in the fragrant aroma when Varley opened the front door and stood aside to let her enter first. "It ain't a mansion but it's home," she said. "And we're free to come and go as we please without havin' to ask permission from the master."

"You and your family live here then?" Douglass asked.

"Me and my husband and two kids, we take that room." Varley pointed toward a doorway leading into a spotless room where Douglass could see a bed covered with a patchwork quilt.

"My momma and my younger sister, they live in that room," Varley pointed the other way to another room, "and my husband Benjamin's brother, he sleeps in this room. Momma does cookin' at the cafe right next to the depot. My sister, she washes up the dishes, and cleans rooms, dependin' on what they want her to do. My husband works down at the docks on the river, and I take in sewing so I can be here with Olivia. Most of the time I can keep her out of trouble. Now let's set up to the table and have us some coffee and cookies."

The middle room served as both living room and kitchen, as well as a bedroom for Benjamin's brother. The table set toward the back of the room, the whole house was scarcely as big as Douglass' bedroom at the ranch in DeKalb.

"Let me help." Douglass removed her hat and followed Varley into the kitchen.

"Okay, then you put the cookies on that plate and I'll set the coffee to heatin'. You take cream or sugar?" Varley asked.

"No, I like it plain." Douglass ate two oatmeal cookies while she arranged a dozen others on the tray. They were even better than those that the cook made at her home and she found herself hoping that Varley's mother made some for the cafe where she cooked. It had to be the same place Monroe had mentioned taking her for supper.

"Me too. Ain't no use in doctoring up something good as

black coffee. Now tell me what is it you're doing in Memphis."

Douglass entertained her for more than an hour with the story of how she'd been left beside the road and what had happened since then. Varley laughed so hard when Douglass told about her brothers that she had to wipe the tears from her face on her apron. "Mercy, woman, what you ain't been into ain't been thought up," Varley said. "I'm right glad you rescued my Olivia. Seems like I been needin' a good afternoon like this. When you come through here on your way back to Texas, you stop in again. You can stay with us if you'd like. Me and Benjamin, we'll sleep on the floor in this room and give you our room."

"Why, thank you, Varley," Douglass said. "That's right generous and I might take you up on the offer."

Monroe was pacing the sidewalk by the time she returned. For more than ten minutes he'd been sure she'd disappeared and there was an emptiness in his heart he didn't even want to think about. He didn't really care what happened to her . . . or did he? When he looked up and saw her meandering back down the sidewalk toward the depot, one part of him wanted to run as fast as he could to meet her while the other part wanted to give her a piece of his mind.

The latter part won.

"Where have you been? I told you to be here at five sharp and it's almost a quarter past. We'll have to order some food and have it packed now. There won't be time for a proper meal," he almost shouted.

"Don't you raise your voice to me, Monroe Hamilton. I had a wonderful time with a lady, having cookies and coffee. That old witch down the street refused to let the little child in her store because she's a freed slave and so the mother invited me home with them and I went."

"Good Lord, you've been over there in that part of town!" Monroe gasped. "Don't you know how dangerous that is. If anything would have happened to you it could have incited another riot. There was a horrible one in May. More than forty black people were killed, seventy others injured. There's a movement called the Ku Klux Klan in these parts and they're waiting for an excuse to hang or kill black people. If you'd been hurt in any way, they'd have used it to cause an uprising," he whispered hoarsely.

"Well, it didn't," she said. "Now while you order food I'm going down to the Irishman's store at the end of the block and buying a few hairpins. And if they have oatmeal cookies, tell them to put some in the basket. Varley's momma cooks in that cafe and she makes the best I've ever eaten."

Douglass was sitting in the coach ready to go when Monroe shoved a big basket of food inside and joined her. His heartbeat was almost back to normal, but his mind was in a whirl, wondering why on earth he cared enough about the woman to be so upset.

"What is that?" he asked when he got situated, his hat on one side of the bench, the basket on the other.

"Pillows," she told him, rolling her eyes toward the ceiling. "I bought them at the Irishman's store. He didn't have any pillow cases so we'll have to use them like this, but it might make the sleeping a little more comfortable."

Monroe chuckled. "Nothing is comfortable when you're trying to sleep in a bouncing stage coach."

He was a prophet, pure and simple, she decided when darkness fell and she tried in vain to get comfortable. First she propped the pillow against the side and leaned into it, then she tried lying on the bench only to find herself tumbling toward the floor when the wheels fell in a rut.

"Why don't you make the floor your bed?" Monroe asked. "I can manage to catch a few winks propped on the side if I can stretch my legs out and put them on your seat. I've slept in worse conditions."

Douglass had to pull her knees up and tuck them under the bench where he sat and endure the sight of his legs slung up six inches from her midriff, but it sure beat the other ways she'd tried to sleep.

"Monroe, the first time you saw me out there on that road sitting on my trunk, did you think I was an octoroon?" she asked.

The question startled him. Great glory! If anyone thought that, then she wouldn't be allowed in restaurants or some stores. Had that woman at the store in Memphis accused her of being an octoroon?

"You asleep or are you going to answer me?" she asked drowsily.

"No, I didn't think you were an octoroon," he said honestly. "I didn't think anything. All I saw was a pretty lady with the most gorgeous eyes I'd ever seen."

"Thank you," Douglass said quietly. Had Monroe Hamilton really paid her a compliment? Or was he covering up his own ideas? What would the rest of the trip be like if she encountered others like that woman? Suddenly, she smiled at the soft tone he'd used when he said that about her eyes. So Monroe thought she had lovely eyes, did he? Well, he didn't have any idea how his dark brown eyes and all that black hair, on his head as well as his chest, affected her. And he'd never know. There wasn't a Yankee mother in the whole United States of America who'd want her son tangled up with a woman who folks thought was an octoroon.

The stage rocked on for another hour before Douglass finally went to sleep. It was a long time before Monroe finally quit thinking about Douglass Sullivan's eyes.

Chapter Eight

"I ain't lettin' no lady ride in an empty car," the stocky engineer declared. "Ain't no way. I might let you go in it, but a lady's got to have proper things."

The muscles in Monroe's jaw flexed as he ground his teeth. He could either continue the journey on a slow moving stage with Douglass beside him, or he could send her on to Philadelphia with no chaperone and take the train by himself. Neither option appealed to him. She'd ridden two nights in the stage, sleeping on the floor, eating cold food from baskets prepared wherever the stage stopped for five or ten minutes, even chasing behind a bush without complaint. Even when boredom set in or when other passengers crowded against her, she didn't whine. The only sigh that escaped her mouth was that very morning when she said she'd love to have a real bath.

"What if I told you she wasn't a lady but an octoroon?" Monroe asked.

"That'd make a difference for sure." The man grinned lewdly. "Taking a little enjoyment along with you on your trip back home, are you? Why didn't you tell me the real situation when you come in here? The empty car is the fifth one back. It's clean as a pin and I expect to find it that way when we stop in Nashville. That'll be five dollars for the both of you. Mind what I say, no half-eaten food stinkin' up the car, and make sure you find a place outside the car when we make our stops. If I find anything like that in the corners I'll shoot you and keep the octoroon for myself. Understood?"

"Yes, sir." Monroe handed the man a five-dollar gold piece and went back to the tiny, brick, one-room rail station. "We've got a place in an empty car. I'm sorry this isn't a passenger train but it'll go faster than the stage coaches and get us to Nashville much quicker," he told Douglass, who'd been waiting patiently, sitting on a bench under a huge old maple tree, shedding its brilliant burgundy leaves, some filtering down to lay in her lap.

"Pillows?" she asked.

"Yes, and your trunk. Is there enough room for my saddlebags inside the trunk?" he asked.

"Sure, what about a bed roll? It is an empty car isn't it?"

"Yes, it is. But the man said it's clean. We'll see what we can find. We've got an hour to get a food basket packed and get loaded. You sure you're up to this, Douglass?" he asked.

Well, would wonders never cease? The good captain actually sounded like he cared whether she could endure a leg of the journey in an empty railroad car. Holy smoke, she'd slept two nights in a bouncing stage coach. Compared to sharing that small of a space with Monroe so close, a huge railroad car would seem like the whole floor of a hotel.

"We've got a lot to do in an hour." She nodded. "And I can have a bath tomorrow night in Nashville?"

"I promise," he said.

They'd finished loading their things into the box car when the engineer tapped on the door and asked Monroe to step outside. Hoping the man hadn't pocketed the money he gave him and then intended to throw them off the train like vagabonds, Monroe stepped out cautiously.

"I found out some disturbing news, Mr. Hamilton," the man said in a low voice. "I'll pass it on to you and you do what you must. It might be a good place to get rid of that bit of fluff you're traveling with. Just leave her in Nashville if you've a mind to get rid of her without anyone ever know-

ing. It's your decision and all. But there's been a cholera epidemic in Nashville this summer. 'Pears they might have gotten it under control since the deaths have slowed down
somewhat. Had about eight hundred die so far. Anyway we
ain't stoppin' there 'cept to unhitch a car load of medical
stuff back there. Take about ten minutes at the most. If'n I
was you and had a mind to do so, I'd unload the woman and
leave her there. What happened next would be 'twixt her and
the Good Lord," he said.

"And where does this train go on past that?"

"Line ends out east of there in Algood," the man said.

"How much would it take to get on that far?" Monroe
asked.

"Another five ought to do it," the man said, his beady little eyes shifting from one place to another.

Monroe dug in his pocket and brought out another gold
piece. "You stopping for anything anywhere between here
and there?"

"One car load comes off in Camden," he nodded, pocketing the money.

"I need to send a telegram to Nashville and have someone
meet me at the train. That possible?" Monroe asked.

"Sure is. It's the first stop we make. 'Bout supper time tonight. Telegraph office is right there in the depot. Be easy for
you to get it sent if you work fast. Leave that woman in the
car though. Looker like her would cause a problem, I'm
thinkin'," the man said.

"Yes, sir, and thank you," Monroe said.

The man nodded. Didn't make him no never mind what
Mr. Hamilton was thanking him for. Advice was advice.
Take it or leave it. But the engineer wouldn't be a bit sur-
prised when he got to the end of the line to find Mr.
Hamilton traveling a lot lighter than he was when he rented
that box car.

Monroe found Douglass flipping out a blanket on one side
of the eight-foot car. It would soon be dark and she planned

to sleep stretched all the way out that night. She'd ridden a train once before and compared to a stage that hit every single rut and hole in the road, she'd feel like she was being rocked to sleep in the bosom of a nanny. She glanced up at him, but didn't say a word. One more night, and sometime tomorrow evening they'd be in Nashville where a fancy hotel and lots of hot water waited. What was it the Bible said? Those that endure until the end shall be saved. Well, she'd endure until tomorrow to be able to sink down deep in a tub filled to the brim with warmth. She didn't intend to waste a single bit of that heat either. She'd stay submerged until the water was cold as clabber.

The train burped then roared to life. She was thrown off balance when the train cars creaked and found herself in a tangle of petticoats, hat askew, and freshly-made blanket bed all crumpled up in the corner. Cool fall air whistled through the door Monroe had left ajar for lighting purposes. She shook her head, dislodging a dozen or more hair pins. The train was running smoothly now, and she figured she could keep her balance if she got up and began her tasks all over again.

"Kind of snuck up on you, didn't it?" Monroe asked above the clackedy-clack of the wheels running on the tracks. "It's not as nice as a plush passenger coach."

"No, it's not, but it's a bit roomier than a stage and it's only for a night and a day," she said.

An uneasy feeling invaded Monroe's heart. To tell her now would be to get her used to the idea. To wait until later wouldn't help matters. Oh, but he did hate to suffer the look in her eyes when she realized she was going still yet another day passed that for her bath.

"You know I made you a promise a little while ago?" he began.

She eyed him, drawing her dark brows down in a ridge over blue eyes that were already shooting sharpened daggers at him. "And you are going to keep it, right?" she asked.

"I can." He nodded. "We can get off this train in Nashville. Nothing says we can't. But there's been a cholera epidemic the past few months in Nashville. Eight hundred people have died. I've paid the man to let us stay on the train to the end of the line in Algood. We can have a night in a hotel there, catch a coach to Huntsville and I think there is a proper passenger train there that will take us a bit farther."

She almost wept, but somewhere down in the depths she found an inner core of strength. But what was she going to do about Colum and Flannon? What if they rode right into Nashville and were stricken with cholera? She'd never, ever forgive herself if she caused either or both of them to die because of her impetuosity. Surely by the time Colum tracked her to Memphis and then to Jackson he'd realize there were no tickets bought on the stage. It wouldn't be so very difficult to find the man who'd taken money to let them ride in an empty box car and he'd tell them his passengers had ridden to the end of the line. There didn't seem to be one thing she could do but hope Colum was really the expert tracker everyone said he was.

"Decision?" Monroe pulled a string and unrolled his own bedroll, which he bought at the last minute in a general store, with a flick of the wrist, threw one of the pillows she'd purchased in Memphis at one end and stretched out.

Seeing him there, with his ankles crossed and his hands laced behind his neck was enough to give her a case of hives. A bath surely wasn't worth worrying about him catching cholera and then watching him die a painful death. She walked gingerly over to the open door and watched the scenery speed past her at a breathtaking pace. Not even riding her favorite horse across the wide open spaces of north Texas, her hair blowing behind her and her skirt tails threatening to fly all the way to heaven, had afforded her such a buzz of excitement. The cool fall air blowing against her face and the exhilaration of knowing she was outwitting her two brothers, even if it was a day at a time, was absolutely thrilling.

"I suppose we have no choice but to go on a while longer," she said, not trusting herself to look at Monroe. "But how are you going to deliver your papers?"

"I'm sending a telegram from a stop along the way. My contact in Nashville will meet the train, take my papers and give me theirs to take on to Washington D.C. I'll have him bring another basket of food and some boiled water for drinking." Monroe carefully let out the pent up air he'd been holding in his lungs, but he didn't face the demon in his heart. One that had come to respect Douglass Sullivan far more than he wanted to admit.

They shared half a loaf of bread, cold ham, and cheese for supper. Douglass didn't even flinch when he handed her a quart jar filled with water and his fingertips brushed against hers. Neither the noise of the train's wheels nor the whirr of the wind as it blew through the door could possibly sound as loud as her heart pounding against her rib cage. There she was, sweaty and disheveled from not having a mirror in two days to even groom herself, her traveling suit wrinkled and dusty, and she actually cared what Monroe thought of her.

Mary, Mother of Christ, she thought, carefully helping repack the basket. Breakfast and lunch tomorrow would be more of the same, but she did see some cookies hiding in one corner. Even those didn't combat the rampant thoughts jumping around in her head. *He's as smelly and dirty as I am and still makes my heart skip a beat. If I hadn't sworn off all men, I'd swear I was beginning to like the man. And why shouldn't I? He's been a gentleman and he's taken care of me. But he'll be so glad to get back to his Love's Valley he'll probably dance a jig that he's rid of a woman who everyone in this part of the world thinks is a woman of color.*

"Whatever are you thinking about? You look like you could commit a murder and not even have nightmares about it," Monroe said, interrupting her thoughts. She was so beautiful standing there with the last light of evening filtering in through the crack in the door. Half her face was in shadow, the other half illuminated by the fast fading glow of the setting sun.

"Nothing. I'm tired and sleepy. Do we have to stay awake until it's full dark or can we curl up in our blankets now? And is it all right for me to remove my shoes?" she asked, already smoothing out her blanket and fluffing up the caseless pillow.

"You can sleep right now if you want. All the way until morning or noon if you think you can." He grinned. "And you can take off or put on anything you want. The train will make a stop at first light in that little town I mentioned. I'll send a telegram from there. I expect you'd better make use of the outhouse behind the depot, and please try to do it carefully. The engineer did say he didn't want us using the car for that purpose. But he also didn't want anyone to know he'd let us ride in the empty car."

"Don't be vulgar, talking about outhouses and such," she said, stifling a yawn. "I'm taking the side closest to the door."

"Don't fall out," he cautioned. His own conscience pricked his soul to the very core. "Douglass, I've got a confession. There's another reason you need to stay hidden away as much as possible."

"I expect I need to go to confession too, soon as we find one," she said sleepily.

"No, I think you should know that I had a hard time getting the engineer to let us have this car. He thought you were a lady of some standing and said ladies didn't ride in empty cars like vagabonds," Monroe told her.

"And?" Douglass raised an eyebrow and propped herself up on an elbow.

"I told him you were an octaroon. I'm sorry I had to lie. Oh, and don't get so close to the doors or you'll fall out."

"You told that man I was an octaroon!" she exclaimed. "Is that what you really thought when you found me sitting on the trunk?"

"No, it isn't, but we need to get to Washington. The papers I have are very important and the president needs them. I feel bad about it, but I wanted you to know, because he's going to treat you different," Monroe said.

"Hush! I don't want to talk about it," she whispered, moving her bed back a foot father into the car. Inhaling the nice evening air, she shut her eyes. This was definitely better than the floor of the bouncing stage coach. Her mother would literally lay down and die if she knew what Douglass was doing. Sleeping in the same boxcar as Monroe. Traveling along as fast as they could in whatever conveyance they could find. Nice women didn't travel with men like Captain Monroe Hamilton even if he was a nice person, not unless they were married. He was a Yankee, a handsome one, but a Yankee nonetheless. She didn't want to spend the rest of her life locked up in a convent. She wanted to live a full, happy life. To marry some day, have a yard full of children and a house of her own, horses to train, flowers to grow, and a man to wrap her arms around in the night when the storms of life surrounded her. Someone the exact opposite of that weasel, Raymond Pierce. Someone who hadn't thought she was an octoroon deep down in his heart. She fell asleep conjuring up visions of Raymond, his pale little mustache dropping down over his mouth as she slung a rope around his neck and slapped the flanks of the horse he sat upon.

Sometime in the night the train made a wide sweeping curve to the north and the door of the boxcar slid open a bit farther. The night air had turned downright cold and Douglass pulled the blanket tighter around her chilly body, tucking the ends up under her neck. The door continued to slide an inch or two at a time until it was fully open. Douglass shivered but didn't awaken fully. She rolled over once, trying to keep the crisp wind out of her face. The side next to the hard floor planks began to cramp so she flipped over to the other side in her sleep.

She dreamed she was running from Colum. The wind whipped her long braids back and forth across her face. Looking over her shoulder, she saw him gaining on her, so she darted into the barn and shimmied up the ladder into the hay loft. She thought she'd lost him and stifled a giggle, but then she could hear his boots clomping as he stormed up the ladder and into the loft after her. She began to back up, begging him to go away and leave her alone. His dark Mexican eyes glittered with anger and she knew even in the dream that he hadn't softened one bit. Suddenly, he rushed forward and she fell backwards out of the loft.

For a moment before she awoke, she really thought it was all a dream. Then her eyes popped open at the same time Monroe's hands clamped down over hers. Like a flag blowing in the fierce Texas wind, her body flopped one way and the other, the ground under her going by so fast it terrified her. Her bare feet didn't quite reach the gravel piled up beside the railroad ties, but little pieces of rock kept hitting them, letting her know that she was only inches from skinning every bit of skin off her feet and legs.

"Help me!" she screamed.

"I'm trying," Monroe yelled back. "I'm going to pull you inside."

The whole incident lasted less than a minute. One second he heard a muffled scream; the next he was reaching out for her as she tumbled through the doors and out of the car. He wondered even as he fought the wind and the speed of the train, dragging her back inside the cabin, how he had gotten from one side of the boxcar to the other so fast. Sixty seconds that seemed like sixty minutes of pure living torture. She could do nothing to help him, the way her body was being whipped around like a scarf in the wind.

An eternity passed, and her whole life flashed before her eyes before he gave a final tug and she landed halfway across the car with him on top of her. She inhaled deeply, filling her tortured lungs with Tennessee night air, glad to be alive. Then she opened her eyes to find him staring down at her. He'd propped his muscular body up on his elbows and was gasping for wind like she was.

The tableau lasted a lifetime.

She was alive and apparently unharmed, but his heart still raced like a thoroughbred given the reins to run full out. He didn't want her, he kept repeating to himself, but he didn't want her dead.

Those dark eyes, so sensual, so deep there was no bottom, bore into hers with such intensity, she thought she'd drown in them. Death had given her a full-fledged kiss on the lips and Monroe had saved her life. She reminded herself that he would have done the same for a mangy mutt or an octoroon even, but her heart wasn't listening.

Douglass shut her eyes before his lips found hers. A strange mixture of emotions rattled through her body when his tongue flicked across her mouth. He deepened the kiss and she couldn't have stopped him if the alternative would have been standing before a firing squad. She wrapped her arms around his neck and pulled him closer, not caring about society's rules and regulations.

Nothing in her life had prepared her for the effect of that kiss. Her knees were weak and it wasn't all due to the close brush with death. Warmth enveloped her body and she wanted to lay there forever letting him move his mouth on hers like that.

Monroe's heart literally hummed. Then he came to his senses. He hadn't meant to kiss Douglass. It was the heat of the moment. She was alive. He'd saved her. They needed to prove they weren't dead. It didn't mean a thing.

"I'm sorry," he said suddenly, jumping up and slamming the door shut, blocking out all light. He sat down in darkness, a sliver of the early morning sunshine sliding through the crack between the two doors.

"Why?" she asked, sitting up, taking stock of her bones. Nothing was broken. There's be bruises tomorrow, but nothing that wouldn't heal. Not anything like what would have happened if he hadn't grabbed her as she fell. All of her skin was still intact. Her mouth felt a bit swollen as she brushed her fingertips across it. And warm; it felt warm. She was surprised it wasn't downright scalding.

"I shouldn't have kissed you. I was wrapped up in the moment. I've heard people respond to near death experiences like that. Strangers falling into each other's arms to make sure they are really alive," he reported stoically, not believing a word he said.

"Well, I'm not sorry," Douglass said. "I enjoyed it immensely. Not that I'd have you think I'm a woman who is free with her affections. It was the best kiss I've ever had."

"Oh, and you've had so many you can make comparisons?" he asked icily.

"That's for me to know and you to find out." She laughed. "If you'll toss my blanket back over here, I think I could sleep a while longer."

He kicked it across the boxcar to her, not trusting himself to carry it over there. If his fingers touched hers again, he'd lose control. And Monroe Hamilton didn't intend for that to ever happen again. He'd be the gentleman he was brought up to be. Deliver her to her aunt and then go home to Love's Valley. In a few weeks, he'd forget all about the reaction his entire body had to that one kiss.

Douglass had another lie to own up to when she finally found a church where she could go to confession, because with the warmth of his kiss still on her lips, there was no way she could go to back to sleep. A smile tickled the corners of her mouth and she was glad it was dark enough that he couldn't see her. She turned her back to make sure. With his already inflated ego he sure didn't need to know how she planned to garner another kiss or two before she bid him good-bye in Philadelphia. She'd sure enough enjoyed that kiss. Raymond had never made warmth penetrate every fiber of her being.

Douglass hoped that when she found a husband he made her feel exactly like that.

Chapter Nine

They concluded the journey in the boxcar, then traveled on stagecoach for days until Monroe could purchase tickets on a passenger train somewhere in Virginia. The past fifty-five miles, from Richmond, Virginia to Washington D.C., they'd traveled by steamboat. The evening aboard the boat was romantic, the night air cool and sweet. Douglass had stayed in seedy hotels, fancy hotels, and slept on stagecoach floors as well as her own personal little room on the steamship. She'd seen brilliant sunsets on the far horizon, a straight line separating land and sky. Her breath caught in a gasp when she peeked out the coach window and realized how high she was in the mountains of Virginia. For weeks she'd traveled with Monroe, but they had yet to share another kiss.

Douglass stood in front of an enormous round mirror above a shiny oak vanity in her elaborate hotel room and wished she'd been one of those women who had attended the Rights Convention in May of that year. She'd read about it in a five-month-old newspaper she found lying in the bottom of a drawer. Would those women advocate brazenness in women? If so, Douglass would put her name on the line and join up with them because she'd surely like to wrap her arms around Monroe Hamilton's neck and see if all his kisses were as wonderful as the first one. But even though she'd thrown caution to the wind when she began traveling with the Yankee, she couldn't bring herself to take the first step and initiate another kiss.

Rejection, she thought as she checked her reflection. Abulita told her that the reason the young swans in and around DeKalb didn't come right out and ask for her hand in marriage was because they were afraid the answer would be no. Well, men sure didn't have the monopoly on the rejection commodity. Women were afraid of it too. Rejection often meant heartbreak, and women would rather live with a dream imbedded deeply in their hearts than suffer the heartbreak of having nothing.

"My, my, don't you look lovely," Monroe said.

Douglass jumped but managed to cover the way he affected her senses by tucking an errant strand of straight black hair back into the bun at the nape of her neck.

"Thank you," she said. Monroe's reflection in the mirror had swiftly brought her back from the land of dreams to reality, and in the real world he was even more handsome than when he was absent from her sight. Whoever coined that silly phrase about being out of sight and out of mind hadn't ever met or been kissed by Monroe Hamilton, she thought.

As if it were alright to stare unabashedly in a mirror, he looked his fill. Exotic was the only word to describe her. The simple white evening dress, embroidered around the hem with red roses, enhanced the toasted color of her flawless skin. A wide ruffle of some kind of transparent fabric worn off her shoulders made his fingers want to touch her neck and shoulders, to bury his face in the sensitive, soft skin and string kisses from there to her full mouth. Monroe shook the image from his mind and cleared his throat. She'd never be interested in a plain old Yankee. No, not this exotic flower. She was cut out for nights of dancing and holding court in the hot summer nights of Texas. When had he figured out that he even liked her? he wondered. Was it the night of that wonderful kiss in the boxcar? Or had his feelings developed slowly from hate to toleration to like? From there could it soon be love? *No, sir,* he told himself bluntly. The trip had actually been fun and he wasn't sorry he'd rescued Douglass. Not one bit. At least not after that stunt of stealing his horse. She'd even been downright amusing and amiable these past weeks, but he wasn't about to fall in love with a Texan.

Douglass admired Monroe in his evening attire, ready for the gala party they'd been invited to that evening. The women would flock around him like female cats in heat and she'd have to save him from the onslaught if she ever hoped to entice him into another kiss. She picked up a tall *peineta,* the Spanish hair comb her grandmother had given her for her sixteenth birthday, and placed it just so at the top of the bun. Originally designed to hold the *mantilla,* the top of the filigree work in the tortoise shell peeked above the top of her head, giving the appearance of a royal crown. She frowned at the idea. She might not be an octoroon like that silly storekeeper had thought in Memphis, but she was far from being some kind of Spanish queen.

"That is beautiful!" Monroe busied himself brushing imaginary lint from his shoulders. Anything to keep from gazing at her any longer.

"It's a *peineta,* a comb to hold the *mantilla.* I thought I'd wear it tonight, but then it might be out of place." She picked up the lace piece and threw it over the top of the *peineta.*

"Wear it," he whispered hoarsely. "It's the crowning glory. Such lovely fine lace." He touched the lace-embroidered edge, thinking all the while that it wasn't one bit more lovely or fine than the woman wearing it.

"The floral motifs are called the *puntas de castanuela,*" she explained. "If you really think I should, I might wear it after all. It doesn't look out of place since I'm wearing a white dress, I suppose." She turned this way and that, checking her reflection one last time.

"I couldn't say that if I tried." Monroe smiled.

Her heart stopped. It was a real grin, one that reached his eyes and made them sparkle. She hadn't seen many of those in the weeks they'd traveled together. Most of the time there was a deep sorrow in his dark eyes, one that he never talked about but that seemed to live in his heart and soul.

"It's Spanish. Abulita—that's my grandmother—still speaks it more than English. We picked up the language growing up right next to her. I suppose I'm ready. Are you sure this is alright to wear to a formal evening at the White House?" she asked a bit nervously, pulling on her globes.

"I'm very sure." Monroe offered his arm.

A hired buggy delivered them to the edge of the lawn and they strolled past the new fountain installed the year before on the south lawn of the White House. The evening air was exhilarating to Monroe, but not as much as the feeling in his heart when he stepped through the ballroom doors and saw the look on everyone's faces as they turned toward the newly arrived couple.

A stilled silence filled the room and Martha Patterson, the hostess for the evening, as well as President Andrew Johnson's daughter, greeted them warmly. "Captain Monroe Hamilton," she said, holding her hand out gracefully. "And this would be your cousin by marriage that you mentioned this afternoon. I do believe I see some Spanish here. You never told me you had Spanish blood."

"I don't. She is my cousin by marriage. It's very complicated. It is her aunt that is Spanish and my uncle several times removed that married her aunt. But, yes you do see Spanish," Monroe said. "This is Douglass Sullivan from DeKalb, Texas. Her mother is of Mexican descent and her father is Irish. That's where the blue eyes come from."

"I'm so pleased to meet you. Please come on inside and meet the other guests. Father will be glad to meet you as well. He's from Tennessee and traveled to Texas in his youth," Martha said.

"I'm glad to make your acquaintance too," Douglass demurred. Yes, she did know President Johnson was from

Tennessee. She'd heard her grandfather and father cuss and rant about what a traitor he was for staying in the north when Tennessee seceded. Perhaps they'd been wrong, she thought as she laid her arm on Monroe's and let Martha lead the way across the room to meet the greatest man in the United States of America, President Andrew Johnson. After all, she'd been wrong about Monroe. Her first impression when he rode up beside her as she sat in the sweltering Texas heat in the middle of the road was to check to see if he had horns hiding under that jet-black hair. There was no way she'd ever keep company with a Yankee, she had thought, especially so soon after Raymond Pierce had shown his true colors— black and white, like a skunk. But she'd been wrong, judging all Yankees by Raymond. Perhaps there was another story behind why Andrew Johnson stayed in the North. She hoped so, because she was about to be introduced to him and from where she stood right then he didn't have horns or a forked tail either. He was nothing more than a man.

"And may I steal your cousin away for a dance?" President Johnson asked Monroe when the musicians began to play.

"I would be honored," Douglass said, glad the music was something she'd heard before and danced to many times.

"And you are from Texas?" the President asked as he held her at arm's length, going through the steps.

"Yes, sir. A little town in the northern part called DeKalb. We raise horses and do some ranching," she said.

Monroe watched her from the corner of his eye as he listened to Senator Patterson, the President's son-in-law, talk about the new branch of the government called the Secret Service. It's main function was to rout out counterfeiters and put an end to the illegal operations that were wreaking havoc with the economy. Chief William Wood was heading the operation and there was a possibility the new Secret Service would also entail some security for the President and other high government officials.

"Are you listening to me, Monroe?" David asked, a

chuckle erupting from his chest. "Or are you watching that exotic woman you brought tonight under the guise of being a cousin. There's no way that lady is from your family. Sorry, old man, I don't believe it."

Monroe laughed. "It's a long story, but we are really traveling companions. She is fascinating though, isn't she?"

"That is the truth," David said. "But did you hear me talking about the Secret Service?"

"Heard every word. Want me to repeat it back, verbatim?" Monroe asked.

"Well, I wasn't talking to hear my head rattle," David said. "Chief William Wood would like an audience with you at your earliest convenience. Tomorrow morning would be wonderful since you've already delivered the reports today. He's going to offer you a position with the Secret Service."

"And please give my highest regards to William. Tell him I'm honored, but tomorrow morning I shall be gone from Washington D.C. I'm going home, David. Home to Love's Valley to raise horses. If there's any way I can help our country from there then feel free to call on me," Monroe said.

"You're turning down a wonderful offer."

"I'm sure, but I'm tired. I'm going home and do what I like. Raise horses, farm, ranch, pull a living from the land in Love's Valley, Pennsylvania," Monroe told him. "Now I think I shall dance with my cousin since the President wouldn't dare dance with any woman more than once."

"If you change your mind, the offer will still stand," David said.

"Thank you. I will remember that," Monroe said as he crossed the floor and took Douglass in his arms for the next dance.

She fit well inside the circle of his arms, he thought. Dancing together, they looked like they'd practiced for years and both were as cool as cucumbers. It was all a facade though. Her heart tumbled around in her chest so rapidly that she feared the ruffle sitting on her shoulders was pumping up and down.

"Where does one go to get a breath of fresh air?" she asked when the dance ended.

"Right this way." He led her through an open doorway and out onto a verandah.

"Ah, wonderful fresh air." She inhaled deeply. She decided in that moment, while standing so close to Monroe Hamilton, that if she'd had half the nerve she had when she first met him she would lean forward and kiss him soundly on the mouth. She also decided in that moment on the verandah that she was in love with the man. Now all she had to do was convince him that he loved her too. That would be the hardest thing she'd ever have to accomplish.

That and living in the North!

"Monroe, I think I'd better tell you something," she said. Once Douglass made up her mind, she didn't usually worry the issue to death like a blue tick hound dog with a ham bone. She stepped right up and spoke her mind.

"And what would that be, that I stepped on your toes?" He grinned.

She took a deep breath, then a voice from the past shattered her calm reserve.

"Well, look who did find her way to the North after all. Her Mexican majesty has her day in the sun. From the backwoods Texas town of DeKalb all the way to the White House. And who did you have to sleep with to get here?" Raymond leered at her, completely ignoring Monroe Hamilton.

The oxygen in her lungs whooshed out in a gush. Her hands knotted up in tight balls and she battled the urge to blacken both his beady little eyes and break his nose all with one well-placed first. "So we do meet again, and right here at the White House? Imagine them letting skunks like you through the front door. Just goes to show that some folks don't know a rogue when they're looking at him right in the face," she said angrily.

"I don't appreciate you talking about Douglass like that. Would you like to settle this like gentlemen? Say daybreak tomorrow? Your choice of weapons?" Monroe suggested quietly.

"This is my fight, Monroe. If I need your help I'll ask for it, but it don't take much to murder a slimy slug, and that's what Raymond Pierce is. *He's* the Yankee who left me sitting on the side of the road."

Monroe bit the inside of his lip. So this was the culprit he had to thank for all his misery, and good fortune, he admitted. If Douglass didn't freeze him to death with her tone, or kill him outright with those balled up fists, then Monroe resolved that he would take care of the man. If Raymond hadn't intended to marry the woman, he shouldn't have enticed her away from her home and ruined her good name.

"And it sure didn't take you long to find another man who I'm quite sure was a perfect gentleman all these weeks, did it?" Raymond said snidely.

She tilted her chin downward and eyed him from under dark brows knit together in a solid line across the top of her glittering blue eyes. "You must not judge everyone by yourself."

"Well, I see you've met another person." The President was suddenly on her right side. "Let's all step out on the lawn and get some fresh air, shall we? These evenings are necessary, but you know sometimes I miss the little gatherings. Raymond, did you tell these folks that you are working on a newspaper piece about the new Secret Service?"

"No, I didn't," Raymond said. "We hadn't gotten around to that."

Douglass pulled her claws back in, deciding to wait until later to take a real swipe at Raymond. The group stepped out onto the balcony and the President began to tell them about the new branch of the government. Monroe had already heard the news from the President's son-in-law, so he leaned against the wall beside the door and waited patiently. What was it Douglass was about to tell him? That she was ready to go back to Texas, with or without an escort?

Douglass listened intently to the President, or at least appeared to do so. On the outside she was attentive, focused, and serene. Inside, she had no control over a mixed jumble of emotions. She wanted to humiliate Raymond Pierce in front of the President of the United States. She wanted both the President and Raymond to go back inside the White House so she could tell Monroe she'd fallen in love with him. She wanted her heart to stop racing, and she wanted to kiss Monroe and make it race faster.

She got none of the things she wanted.

"Gentlemen and our fair lady from Texas, I suppose we should go back inside so the guests won't think we're out here conspiring," the President said with a chuckle.

"Thank you," Douglass said demurely.

"She's not what you think, Mr. President," Raymond said coldly. "She's not a Spanish queen, you know. Her folks are true-blue Southern Rebels. She has six brothers who fought for the Confederacy. She's half-Mexican and half-Irish."

"And I'd thank you to keep your tongue, Mr. Pierce," the President said softly. "Miss Sullivan is my guest this evening. I don't care if she is Irish or Spanish royalty. All Americans come out of the same melting pot and I'd love to see the day when we have even less of a class system than we do now. Be honorable or go home, young man," President Andrew Johnson said as he went back inside and left the three of them on the balcony.

Douglass smiled, all the tension leaving her heart and soul at one time. "Monroe, I think I'd like another dance now and maybe a cup of punch after that." She looped her arm through his and ignored Raymond. President Johnson had just put him in his place so much better than she could have ever imagined.

"Delighted to be of service," Monroe said very formally.

"You're still not royalty," Raymond pouted.

"No, I'm not," Douglass turned, taking two steps forward until she was nose to nose with him. "I never claimed to be anything other than what I am, Mr. Pierce. 'Twas you who led me on and made illusive promises you had no intentions of keeping. You lived in my home, ate at my table, befriended my brothers. You knew exactly what I was and am still. But I didn't know that men weren't as good as their word and as dishonorable as snakes. You proved that to me. I only have one thing to say to you tonight, now that I've had time to cool my Irish temper. Thank you, Raymond Pierce. Thank you for leaving me sitting on the side of the road all alone and unprotected. Thank you for letting me see your true colors that first night. I'm grateful now for all of it, because all of it combined is what put me in the path of Captain Monroe Hamilton, and he's been everything you are not, which restores my faith in humanity. Goodnight, sir. Like the President said, 'Be honorable or go home.' I'd say you'd better go on home since you aren't capable of honor."

With that she looped her arm through Monroe's, leaving Raymond speechless. They'd barely made it inside the candlelit room when the musicians began playing a waltz and she found herself in Monroe's arms. Right where she wanted to be.

"That was quite a speech," he said, inhaling the rose water scent she'd chosen to wear that evening. "And thank you for the compliment."

"It wasn't just a compliment." She looked up into his eyes. "It was the gospel truth. Every word of it. And I've got a confession to make tonight. Later, tonight. Right now I'm going to enjoy this moment. I may never dance in the White House again in my lifetime. Who would have ever thought a Southern Rebel, half-Irish, half-Mexican, would be dancing and visiting with the President of the United States? It all goes to show the President was right."

"Confession? Do we need a priest?" Monroe raised a dark eyebrow.

"Yes, I do. But he'd tell me to do exactly what I'm going

to do anyway," she said. "We'll talk about it when we get back to the hotel. But right now hold me and let me savor this time in your arms."

Savor? Did she really use that word? he thought. *Did she sincerely like being in his arms? And what on earth did Douglass have to confess anyway?* He'd been with her through thick and thin for weeks. Whatever it was, it had to be a minor thing. Nothing, absolutely nothing, could ruin such a perfect evening.

Chapter Ten

Douglass pulled the *peineta* from her hair and carefully folded the *mantilla,* laying both on the dresser. The gig was up, as Colum said when she was in trouble, and it was time for confession. Monroe waited patiently in the open door of the hotel room, his arms folded across his chest, waiting for her to say her piece. Was she about to tell him that she was ready to go home to Texas now? What on earth was on Douglass' mind? What would he do to keep her from going back alone? How far would he go to keep her with him another three days? Questions with no plausible answers tormented his very soul.

Confession.

The word was a big, hard stone in her chest.

If it's confession, then let's do it up right, she thought. She drug a rocking chair across the floor, tangling up a throw rug in the process and nearly swearing as she kicked it out of the way. She situated the chair right at the end of the bed and motioned for Monroe to sit in it. She'd position herself at the end of the bed, the foot board of the bed between them. As soon as she could, perhaps tomorrow, she'd find a real church and go to a confessional. There were so many things she needed to free from her soul: lying, enjoying the sensations of a kiss, deviousness where her brothers were concerned. The list would be long and she'd probably wear calluses on her knees doing penance.

Oh, she loved Monroe Hamilton. She wasn't going to fight that issue at all. She did, plain as the snout on a hog wallowing around in a mud puddle. But loving him and living with him even if he did love her back, which he surely didn't, were two different things all together. She couldn't live in his precious Love's Valley any more than she could sprout wings and fly away to visit with Mary the Mother of Christ. Not really that she couldn't, but more that he would never let her. If some folks thought she was a woman of color then others would, and she'd be an embarrassment to him and his family. She was born and raised to live in Texas, probably right next to her folks, where people knew exactly what she was. Monroe wouldn't ever move south. Not that she could blame him. She didn't want to be a Rebel in the North anymore than he'd want to be a Yankee in the South. The time was horribly wrong and she could have gladly tossed her heart out in the yard for going and falling in love with the most unlikely, unacceptable man on the whole great green earth.

Smiling, he crossed the room and sat down in the rocking chair. Whatever Douglass had to say couldn't upset him. He was too close to home for that. He could shut his eyes and see his mother; red hair shot through with silver these days, dark brown eyes, and a gentle fairness that didn't go with that red hair. Not that she couldn't be stubborn and hard-headed. It had taken that to keep their farm going when his father died and she had stepped right into the job, taking the reins overnight and running things exactly like Harrison Hamilton had done. Ellie, with her long blond hair, clear blue eyes, and the pale English skin she'd inherited from her mother, who still had an accent last time Monroe talked to her. A lump formed in his throat thinking that his aunt and uncle were both dead. Indigo, tall like his mother only twice as stubborn and fiery, with long, long brown hair and eyes the same color as her name: a deep, deep blue. He'd see them all very soon now. In just three days he'd make his last official stop in Philadelphia to deliver the last of the papers in his case and escort Douglass to her aunt. Three days home to Love's Valley. In less than a week he'd be walking through the rustling autumn leaves on his own property, his family all around him in the long evening hours. He couldn't be arriving at a better time. The hay would be harvested, the crops all in. A bit of guilt briefly plagued him as he thought of his mother, sister, and cousin doing all the work, but next year would be so very different. He'd be there for spring planting, from calving season all the way up to the lazier days of fall and winter.

Breaking from his reverie, Monroe raised a dark eyebrow at Douglass, asking when she was going to begin. After all this was her show.

Douglass cleared her throat daintily and perched herself on the end of the bed, the highly-polished oak footboard of the bed between them. She pretended it really was a confessional, only Monroe wasn't a priest. At least she hoped he wasn't.

"Seems like a real confessional, don't it?" she whispered.

"A bit," he said. "But rest assured I'm not a priest, so don't begin this bit of confession with, 'Father I have sinned.' What is it you have to say, Douglass?" he asked, stifling a yawn. "We have a long day ahead of us tomorrow. The first stage leaves before eight o'clock."

"Did you already buy tickets?" She almost groaned.

"No, didn't have time today. Remember, I spent the whole day locked up in the President's personal office, then the whole evening dancing with you. At least when you weren't waltzing with the President or trying to murder Raymond Pierce."

"Good because you aren't going to Philadelphia."

"Oh, yes, I am." He raised his voice slightly, suddenly wide awake. "I've come this far with you. I will escort you to your aunt's farm."

"Monroe, there is no aunt. I don't have an Aunt Hilda. I said that so you wouldn't make me go back to DeKalb," she said, then waited. Seconds lasted hours and turned into eternity.

"Geraldine said she knew your aunt," he said tersely. "She talked about cousins and her best friend."

"Lies. Father, forgive me for I have sinned," she intoned seriously. "I told a good man a lie and then embellished it. Geraldine made up that story because she could see that I'd lied to you and she didn't want me to be sent back to Texas either," she said seriously.

Monroe was on his feet so fast the rocking chair fell backwards with a thud.

"Don't be mad at me, please," she pleaded. "I had to tell you something to get you to take me away from Texas. My brothers are following us. I saw them in Arkansas and they'll be here before long. I can stay right here until they catch up to me and you can go on home."

Monroe rolled his eyes toward the ceiling.

"You have no relatives this side of the Mason-Dixon line?" he asked through gritted teeth. "Nowhere I can take you and leave you for them to find you?"

"None." She shrugged her shoulders.

"Then you are going to Love's Valley with me. When your brothers arrive you will tell them exactly what has happened. I'll not have a bad reputation hanging on my good name because you lied," he said.

"I will not!" She raised her voice an octave and shot off the bed, stomping her foot and pointing her finger at him. "Your family would crucify me, Monroe. They're Yankees and I'm a Rebel. They don't want me in their home and they'll never believe we traveled all that way without . . ." She blushed scarlet.

"Oh, yes, you will. That's your penance, Douglass Sullivan, for being so devious. Your brothers shouldn't be far behind us. We didn't try to cover our tracks so they'll be along in a few days, and you can sit right in my parlor and tell them what a gentleman I've been this whole time."

"You think they're going to believe me?" She slapped at him and he caught her wrist. The tingle from his fingertips touching her bare arm sent a jolt of electricity all the way to the ends of her tired toes.

"Why not? Have you got a reputation for lying or do you just lie to Yankees?" he asked, glaring down at her and wondering all the while what he'd ever thought beautiful about the imp. She was the devil incarnate.

"I have not! And you are not going to force me into going to your precious Love's Valley with you, either. I'm a grown woman. I can make my own decisions," she said.

"Like Raymond Pierce?" Monroe's mouth curved up in a wicked grin, but there was only mockery in it, no amusement.

Douglass jerked her arm free from his hand and turned her back on him. She couldn't stand to see him so mean, and she was not going to his home with him either. "I'm. Not. Going. With. You." She emphasized each word. "And don't you be throwing up one mistake to me, either. Raymond was a bad mistake. That's all."

"You have no choice. You owe me that much for lying to me, Douglass." His hand was on the door knob. "Your brothers will know about the night we spent in the brothel. They'll know about the train boxcar and heaven only knows the newspapers will mention our names concerning tonight at the White House. They'll be out for blood, shooting first and asking questions later, so you're going home with me to keep me from dying. I lived through the war and I'm not ready to lose everything because some little tart lied to me."

She wanted to kick something, preferably Monroe. He was right and she hated being wrong.

"Besides they won't really crucify you. I'll send a telegram tomorrow letting them know I'm bringing a house guest and they'll be excited about company. We don't have a lot of guests situated where we are back between two mountain ridges. It's only after we get there and I tell them the whole story that they will give you the cold shoulder. It's no more than what you deserve, though, now is it?"

"Don't you be condescending to me! I'm not a three-year-old. I'm a survivor, and if it took telling a rotten old Yankee a lie to survive then I'd do it again," Douglass declared. She tapped her foot angrily, but not one bit of the rage seemed to be easing out the bottom of her shoe.

"Then that's settled. We'll be home in three days."

"Three days? I thought you said it was three days to Philadelphia then three more to Love's Valley." She whipped around to face him again, surprised that in the length of time she'd been turned he hadn't grown nubbins on the top of his head.

"It's three days from here if we don't have to go to Philly," he said. "Be ready to go at six in the morning. We'll eat breakfast in the dining room and I'll buy tickets at the station for the first stage headed north."

"Six," she groaned.

"Yes, and get used to it. Hamiltons don't lie about in the mornings. We're up before the crack of dawn and working," he said.

"I'm not a Hamilton," Douglass smarted back at him.

He gave her an insulting grin and shut the door behind him.

She fell back on the bed in a flurry of petticoats and drawers. *Lord have mercy on my soul,* she thought. *Those people are going to hate me.*

Yes they are, and you deserve it, her conscience rebutted.

"Hush," she said aloud as she buried her face in the pillow. Of all the possible scenarios she'd planned in her mind throughout the course of the evening, going all the way to Love's Valley, Pennsylvania was not a part of any one of them. The pillow cases had been changed while she was gone and smelled sweetly of the fall air they'd been dried in. "Well, it'll be the last sweet thing I see or smell for a long time. By the time those Yankee women get through with me a convent might look wonderful," she muttered to herself.

"Oh, and by the way," the door slung open and Monroe filled it, "by the time you spend a week in Love's Valley, you might look forward to wearing a nun's habit for the rest of your life."

She threw a pillow at him, hitting him square in the face. "Get out of my room and don't come back," she shouted, not caring that the hour was late and there were people up and down the hall trying to sleep.

"Is that all you've got to say, then, because if it is you can get up and lock this door. I was on my way down for a pitcher of warm water when I thought I'd check your door and you'd forgotten to lock it. Are you leaving it open in case Raymond comes sneaking in here? Still laid up over there pouting, are you?" he asked.

Her eyes shot daggers at him. Was he joking or still being condescending? Maybe there was a tad bit of warmth replacing the icy chill in his voice before he left in a huff before. It didn't matter. She'd do her atonement in the middle of a bunch of mountains and go home where she belonged, and she'd hold her head up like a true Sullivan while she did it. They would hate her, but she wouldn't let it affect her. By the time Colum and Flannon arrived, they'd respect her even if they didn't like her.

"No, it's not all I've got to say to you, Monroe Hamilton." She was off the bed in an instant and in his face in another, kicking the pillow from between their feet without ever looking down at it.

"Begging won't get you anywhere," he said.

"I'm not begging," she declared. "I was all set to tell you that I'd plumb fallen in love with you. You've been right honorable and a true gentleman. And I did like that kiss and I'd like some more like it. Where I come from women speak their minds, so don't stand there looking like you saw a ghost. But I've changed my mind. I'm not going to tell you I love you. Not after the way you've treated me like something you tracked in the house from the barnyard this evening. Not that I don't love you. I do with all my heart and the way my skin feels when you touch me makes me want to drag you to the bedroom. Call me a wanton, cheap woman, but that's the truth. But I also know that love is like sittin' on a fence. You got two ways to fall. You can fall in love or out of love. I've decided to fall out of love with you, and that's a fact. And it's all I've got to say, so go away and I'll lock the door behind you this time, for sure."

Monroe stood there mesmerized by the dancing lights in her eyes and the declaration she'd made. Great mercy, had she actually admitted she was in love with him? Before he could take a step backwards and close the door, she took one forward, pressing her body so close to his that shivers ran the entire length of his backbone. Wrapping her arms around his neck, she tiptoed and deftly pulled his mouth down to hers.

The kiss shook the whole hotel. Monroe swore the room swayed in rhythm with the violin music he heard playing somewhere in the distance. He leaned forward when she drew away but she'd already stepped backwards by the time he opened his eyes.

"That is what you messed up," she said. "That is what you could have had the rest of your life. Pretty darned wonderful, ain't it? Well, I can get over it, and you never had it, so there. Go get some sleep. We've got a stage to catch, and I'll tell you one thing more: I can outwork any Hamilton on the face of this earth, so I'll be up at the crack of dawn with the rest of you. When my brothers come to rescue me, I'll tell them the truth and go home to Texas. And I hope you can't ever find anyone who can make you feel like that kiss did. Goodnight, Monroe." She pushed him out the door and slammed it shut, sliding the deadbolt home loudly.

Chapter Eleven

Monroe hid behind a newspaper the whole morning. He didn't know why Douglass had said those things about being in and out of love with him. Most likely, it was merely because they'd spent so much time together and she was mistaking it for something deeper. In the war, friendships among the men were like that. People of all walks of life as well as races were thrown together to work as a team. They came to depend on each other for their very lives and a certain camaraderie blossomed. He and Douglass had been together for several weeks now, on a daily and nightly basis. She had simply mistaken a budding friendship for love. Even though those two kisses had sent his senses reeling, he wasn't so immature or silly as to think they constituted love. It had been years since he'd been around a woman for any length of time. It was purely a case of simple infatuation on both their parts. No one could deny the fact that Douglass Esmerelda Sullivan was attractive, and his body had merely responded in the only way it knew how.

Now she sat across from him in the close confines of the stagecoach, another woman sitting beside her, and all she'd done was throw looks his way that should have set the newspaper on fire and fried him into nothing but a greasy spot on the floor of the stage. Thank goodness for the woman and her chaperone who had boarded at the same time they did. A stiff-necked young lady with a habit of looking down her crooked nose at Douglass every time she wiggled, she hadn't spoken since they left and that was hours ago. Even if the woman was uppity and treating Douglass like she was beneath her, Monroe was grateful to have her on the stage. Douglass wouldn't spout off any more of that talk about being in and out of love with him in front of complete strangers.

From the dark circles under Douglass' eyes, it didn't appear that she'd slept well after her night of confessions. As for him, he'd slept wonderfully. So she was falling out of love with him instead of staying in love with him? Well, that was a relief. He didn't want some little Southern belle, with Irish and Mexican blood flowing in her veins, to be in love with him. He didn't want to hurt her feelings or break her heart even if she had lied to him. He only prayed her brothers wouldn't waste any time and take her off his hands so his life could get back in the familiar rut he was used to. At least that's what he kept telling himself all day.

Douglass gritted her teeth. Her brothers had declared that women folk were temperamental and unpredictable. Evidently they'd never had dealings with a former Yankee officer. Talk about temperamental! He had to know she hadn't slept well, yet there he was pounding on her door before 6:00 that morning. Then of course he acted like nothing had happened, as if they'd planned all the way from that first meeting in Texas that they would go to Love's Valley together. All fine and good for that sorry scoundrel; he was going home a hero to the outstretched arms of his mother, cousin, and sister. He surely wasn't thinking of her and the way those three Yankee women were going to treat her. She'd probably be facing cold tension that would freeze a lesser woman to death. She resolved that she wouldn't let them intimidate her. After all, it was only for a week at the most. Colum and Flannon would be there in a week, maybe less.

The only thing she could do would be to stay out of all those Yankees' way. She shifted her weight to ease the numbness in her bottom. By the time she got home to

DeKalb she would be determined to never ride on a stage again. If they ever got a transcontinental train going she might travel that way. At least they went fast and there was more room. The woman sitting beside her sighed heavily and shot her another mean look. She'd like to strangle the hoity-toity woman and kick that chaperone halfway across Texas. A smile tickled the corners of Douglass' mouth just thinking of the reaction either of the women would have if they came face to face with a coyote or maybe a big coiled up rattle snake. No, the worse thing she could wish upon them would be a tarantula. A spider as big as a saucer with big old hairy legs. That ought to put some fire in their dull, condescending spirits. Heaven help her if Monroe's female relatives were cut from the same bolt of cloth as these two.

The women got off the stage at the first stop and a man with two rowdy little boys crawled inside with Douglass and Monroe, the latter still keeping himself occupied with the newspaper. The man didn't even greet her with a "Howdy, how you doin', ma'am?" He grunted and gave the boys a mean look which did little to settle them down. Luckily they didn't ask questions like, "Are you really a Rebel?" They poked each other, giggled, pointed out the window, made disgusting burping noises, and finally went to sleep, one leaning against the wall, the other on Douglass.

When they stopped for the evening in Damascus, Maryland, neither Monroe nor Douglass had spoken more than was absolutely necessary all day. Both of them had read every word including the advertisements in two separate newspapers, but neither could remember a single sentence or headline.

"I hope they have a decent hotel," Douglass said, letting Monroe help her from the coach.

He laughed. "This is Damascus, Maryland not Washington, D.C. The only reason there is even a stop here is for the stage to pick up and deliver mail. We'll be lucky to find rooms at all."

Douglass groaned, her muscles ached from sitting so long. "A hot supper?" she asked.

"Possible, not probable," he replied. "We'll see what we can find."

What they found was a single room above the station with an outside entrance. The station keeper had outfitted it with a bed, chair, and washstand and had a few renters each month. What they didn't find was a hot meal. They bought cheese and crackers at the general store, along with several fall apples and a loaf of homemade bread the proprietor assured them had been baked that very morning.

"Mr. Svenson, how are you?" the owner of the store said brightly as Douglass and Monroe were leaving.

"Fine, except that I've traveled all day with those two rowdy sons of mine. Next time they want to visit their grandmother, I'm sending the wife to bring them home. Wasted two whole days when I should have been gathering my apples. If frost gets them, it's going to be her fault that we don't have apple butter for our bread this winter," the man said. "The wife sent me to buy cheese before you close up shop. She's making a nice beef stew for supper and the boys think they need cheese to go with it."

Douglass' mouth watered. She was on the brink of asking Mr. Svenson if she could go home with him for supper. Surely she'd earned that much since she'd let his sweaty son use her for a pillow all afternoon.

"Don't you dare." Monroe read her thoughts and body language when she stopped at the door and looked back at the man longingly.

"What? I won't embarrass you," she declared in a whisper. "But that stew sounds good enough to drop down on my knees and beg for."

"We'll make do. You'll be well fed in Love's Valley," he said.

"Yes, but will my portion have arsenic in it?" she inquired seriously.

He chuckled, a deep resonant sound coming from the bottom of his chest. She didn't see one thing funny about the situation. But if she were truly honest with herself, and she'd sure learned to be since she'd written that naive note in DeKalb all those weeks ago, she'd have to admit that she didn't deserve one whit better than she was getting. Lies only bought her distance from her brothers. Lies were sin and now she had to do penance for telling them. She'd fallen in love with the wrong man at the wrong time because of her lies. She'd been treated like royalty in her little area of the world her whole life and she was fast coming to realize that she was just a human being. Her tall pedestal yanked out from under her, her past, present, and future all torn apart by lies, she was quiet as she sorted through her feelings.

Walking down the street was a sheer luxury after being cooped up all evening. There was barely enough daylight left to see the rich fall colors of the fast falling leaves, the mountains throwing their shadow across the quiet street in the small town, and a lady out in the backyard of one of the houses taking in the last of her laundry. Strange, in the South women washed on Monday and she was sure this had to be Saturday. She frowned, wondering what kind of culture she was headed for anyway.

"And what is that look all about?" Monroe asked when they reached the bottom of the weathered wood steps leading up to their rented room.

"Saturday, that's when folks get the house straightened up for Sunday and bake cookies and fresh bread so the Sunday afternoon visitors will have some refreshments. It's not a day to put out a washing," she said.

"What are you talking about?" He stood back and let her go up ahead of him.

"That lady was taking in laundry," she said.

One thing he could say for Douglass was that she was truly observant. He hadn't even seen the woman, he'd been so engrossed in thinking of that nice beef stew the man in the store had talked about. "Perhaps she's had a sickness and had to get the clothes washed before Sunday. Didn't you ever do anything out of routine in Texas?" he asked.

"Of course." She slung open the door instead of waiting for him to open it for her. "One time I made cookies on Monday. They were hard as rocks and stale by the time the Sunday afternoon visitors came around. I never did that again."

He chuckled again and she took stock of the room. No such luck as two beds tonight. One bed was pushed up against the wall next to a wooden chair with a broken back. There were no curtains on the single dirty window, and no water in the mismatched washbowl and pitcher. The trunk they'd begun to share back about the time of the boxcar incident had been placed at the end of the bed. She threw back the covers and inspected the sheets. They hadn't been line dried that day; possibly not even last week, but they were clean and ironed to perfection. No one had slept on them since they'd been washed even if they did smell a bit musty. She poked at the pillows and pushed at the mattress with her palm. Both were feather-filled and calling her name.

"The bed is mine. You can have as much of the floor as you choose to lay claim to," she said, taking off her hat and tossing it in the middle of her bed.

"I don't think so," Monroe said. "I'm sleeping in that bed tonight."

"And you call yourself a gentleman?" She raised an eyebrow as he set about laying out their supper on the broken chair.

"Gentleman or not, I'm sleeping in that bed. You can have the floor." He broke the loaf of bread with his hands and handed her a portion. She bit into it, savoring the rich, yeasty flavor. If she couldn't have stew, at least the store owner hadn't lied about the freshness of the bread. Come morning, if he had another loaf, she intended to buy two of them.

"Cheese?" Monroe asked, slicing it expertly with the knife he pulled from his pocket.

"What did you do with that knife the last time you used it?" Douglass asked.

"Cleaned my toe nails," he said, a grin playing across his handsome face. "Oh, don't look at me like that. I keep my knife cleaner than you keep your hands. I never know what I might need it for."

"You are mean," she said.

How could she ever have thought she loved him? Up until now she'd never believed in all that hocus-pocus about falling in love and going stone blind to a man's faults and failures. That wasn't love; it was absolute insanity. Love didn't erase a man's bad points, it only put them in a place where a woman could endure them. Love? Yes, she did love him, even if he was insisting he have the bed. For one of those hair-raising, heat-seeking kisses, she could be enticed to overlook a lot of things.

Her stomach filled, the newspapers Monroe had bought before leaving Washington read several times over, and dark already settled on the little town of Damascus, Douglass pulled off her shoes and got ready to fight for the bed. "Don't suppose you could be a gentleman and go fill that pitcher with water. Even cold water would be nice to wash my face and hands."

"I can do that, but even if it means I'm not a gentleman, I'm still sleeping in that bed," he said seriously.

As he left with the empty pitcher, she rushed to peel out of her clothes, including the confining corset and under-things and shimmy into the nightrail and matching robe she'd bought in Washington when she purchased the evening gown to wear to the White House. She taken the last pins from her hair, letting it fall in a jet black cascade down her back when he opened the door.

The sight of her standing there sucked every bit of mois-ture from his mouth. He pushed raw desire aside as best he could, set the water on the tiny washstand and, acting as if he thought she looked like an elephant in a ballerina cos-tume at the circus, he sat on the edge of the bed and removed his own boots.

"Cold, but nice," she said, pouring a glassful to drink before she splashed some into the bowl to clean her face and hands. That task finished in a couple of minutes, she pulled the broken chair around to face the window. "Now, it's your turn. I'll keep my back turned until you get your bed made—on the floor."

Monroe didn't even chuckle that time. He gazed his fill of her long black hair cascading down the back of a white night outfit that made her look like an angel descended straight from heaven. Even though he knew better, he could almost see shimmery wings and a golden halo. He slipped out of his shirt, shoved his suspenders down to his hips, and commenced bathing. The cold water did little to calm his frayed nerves, nor did it put out the flames of desire that played havoc with his body.

Douglass hummed a tune as she watched the town fold up for the evening. The general store was already closed and the saloon across the street had little business that evening. Maybe it was busier on the weekends. That's when her brothers went into DeKalb for a beer at the local bar. Her grandmother fussed about it, saying they'd be killed someday hanging out in undesirable places like that, but her father only shrugged and said that boys will be boys. Strange, how boys could break so many rules set up by society and yet girls had to toe the line. No one would send Raymond Pierce to a convent because of his actions.

"Alright," Monroe said, "I'm finished and in bed with the sheet pulled up decently under my chin. Goodnight, Douglass. Sleep well."

"You barn rat!" She hissed when she saw he'd taken the bed after all.

"Even barn rats will look for a soft spot in the hay." He turned his back toward her and his face to the wall. If he had to look at her much longer in that get-up, he'd lose all his intentions to remain a gentleman. He'd surely turn into a blubbering sixteen-year-old again if she pressed up against him in that nightgown and planted one of those earth-shattering kisses on his mouth.

She fumed but only for a few moments. She picked up the chair and put it in the middle of the bed and crawled into the space left on the outside. It might be small, what with his big, muscular body over there against the wall and the chair taking up a good portion of the middle, but it would beat the dickens out of sleeping on the hard floor.

He moaned silently when he felt her weight get into the bed with him. Turning his head slightly, though, he found a chair for a bed partner instead of the sumptuous Irish spit-fire. "What's this?" he mumbled.

"It's a chair. Do Yankees not recognize furniture? It's a chair laid on its side and placed so as to provide a nice break between us," she said.

"Afraid of me? And I was gentlemanly enough to fetch water for you."

"No, Monroe, I'm not afraid of you at all," she said, staring through the rungs of the chair right into his deep, dark eyes. "The chair is not there to protect me from you. You have made it quite clear today that you aren't interested in me. I could have been a complete stranger. As a matter of fact, you were nicer to complete strangers. That's your choice. I told you last night I'd fallen in love with you these past weeks. I'm still working on falling out of love with you. It took a long time to fall in love with you. I don't expect to get the job of falling out of love done in a single day. It will take a while, I'm sure, maybe a whole lifetime. So the chair is not to protect me from you. But rather it is to protect you from me. I'd love another of those kisses and in my half-sleep I might come across this bed and claim it, so the chair will remind me that I'm in the business of falling out of love, not into it. So goodnight, Monroe. You can sleep well knowing that I won't compromise your precious reputation."

With that she flopped over in the bed and left him staring through the rungs at her . . . speechless once again.

Chapter Twelve

Douglass found a flat-nosed shovel in the implement room at the backside of the stables. She'd slept fitfully, in and out of dreams as well as sleep, so she'd finally kicked off the covers, found her britches and shirt in the bottom of the trunk, and went to the stables while the full moon hung low in the sky. Dawn would be pushing it out of sight before long, but by then she'd have the horse stalls cleaned and be back in the house for breakfast—in a dress and looking like a Southern lady should.

Good hard physical labor would take the jitters from her nerves. She'd never dreaded anything so much in her life as meeting Monroe's family. Going home to Texas and facing her own disappointed, upset parents and grandmother was nothing compared to meeting these Yankees. Determined she'd work off the fear, she led a gorgeous horse from the first stable and tethered him to an iron ring hooked onto a support beam at the far side of the barn. Tossing the shovel into a wooden wheelbarrow, she went back to the dirty stable and to the work she was familiar with. She thought about all the lies she'd told to get to where she was that morning, and regret filled her heart. At least in one sense. If she hadn't told those lies, she thought, she would have never known the bottom-falling-out-of-the-world feeling she had deep inside when she kissed Monroe. But he was much too kind and good to have suffered for her own impetuosity. Her parents were probably over their mad spell by now, her brothers would be along any day to rescue her, and this whole adventure would be over. She'd had her adventure, alright. She'd planned on having a wonderful honeymoon and wound up having something even better. The only problem with her adventure was that she'd now be forced to leave her heart in Yankee territory with Monroe Hamilton; all because she'd chosen to tell a bunch of lies. Maybe, just maybe, sometime in the future fate would have thrown them together in a sensible situation and he would have fallen in love with her, but not now. Oh no, not now that he couldn't trust her to tell the truth. She worked harder and faster, but no peace came to her heart.

Douglass and Monroe had arrived in Shirleysburg, the nearest real town to Love's Valley, the previous night at bedtime. She'd thought they'd stay at the small hotel there on Main Street, but not the stubborn Monroe. He could smell his home and wouldn't be kept from it for a few more hours, no matter how tired Douglass was. So he'd rented an open buggy and they'd ridden two and a half miles over the mountain ridge with nothing but the light of the moon to see the rough, rocky road. She had been grateful for the trees lining both sides of the narrow road most of the time. Even though most of them were naked already, at least they managed to fill in the side of the road where the land dropped off into a huge crater. The night air had promised winter was on the way, just as it did that morning, but she hadn't minded too much—not when she was fighting every impulse in her body to keep from chewing her fingernails to the quick.

The house had loomed big, sturdy, and ominous in the pale moonlight. A red brick with two white pillars gleaming by the dim light against all that dark brick. Monroe had driven the carriage he rented around back to the carriage house, and together they'd taken the horses to the barn. The house was dark and everyone had already been asleep for hours, so Monroe had taken her through the back door, into the kitchen, and up a small staircase to the bedroom wing. He carried a candle he'd lit in the kitchen, the flicker of light casting long shadows everywhere she looked. Squeaking ever so slightly, yet sounding like a whining ghost to Douglass, the door he threw open into the bedroom at least had a lock on the inside. They couldn't murder her in her sleep if she kept it bolted securely.

"Sleep well. Tomorrow I won't make you get up at day-break since you're getting to bed so late," Monroe teased, high spirits filling him since he was finally home.

"Oh, hush," Douglass snapped. "I'm sleeping until noon and then after breakfast I'm taking an afternoon nap."

"Tomorrow you may do that. For one day only." He nod-ded, wishing he had the courage to set the candle down and wrap her into his arms for a long hug, but she'd reminded him two nights in a row now that she was in the business of falling out of love with him. The first night she'd put a chair between them in the bed they had shared, yet somehow they'd awakened the next morning with their hands extended through the rungs, their fingertips touch-ing. The next night he'd been able to rent two rooms and he hadn't slept as well as he did sharing the bed with a chair.

"I bet every man who's ever been hung slept like a baby the night before his execution," she murmured as she mucked out the stall. The smell of horse manure mixed with straw and the musty smell of tack from one end of the stables made her think of Texas mornings when she'd done the same job. Even without the warm Texas breezes thrown into the mix, she experienced a pang of homesickness. For the first time she wondered if Colum or Flannon wished they were back in DeKalb mucking out the stables rather than tracking her into Yankee territory. She wondered if her mother thought of her only daughter that morning, and Douglass wished she was in the kitchen with her mother and the cook, preparing enough breakfast to feed an army of brothers and hired help. She owed them all an apology, and she'd deliver it from the heart, not just the lips.

When the stall was clean enough that even Colum wouldn't have found fault with her job, she rolled the wheelbarrow to the back of the stable. The compost pile was located on the opposite side as the one behind their stable in DeKalb, Texas.

"I should've known that," she continued to talk to herself. "Everything will the opposite of the way we do things."

By the time the sun pushed the night away she had the stalls cleaned, and the horses loved, petted, back into their stalls, and fed. Douglass leaned against the double doors at the end of the stable and looked at the huge house sitting at the base of the mountain range and at the long, tree-lined, wagon wheel-rutted pathway that led down to it. From where she stood she could see the mountain range on the other side of the narrow, evidently fertile valley.

"If they flattened all those mountains, this state might be nearly as big as Texas," she said. "How do people live all cooped up in a place like this? Mountains behind them. Mountains in front of them. No sunsets with the sun disappearing down below the flat horizon . . ." She shuddered at the idea.

The house was still dark, so she assumed no one had started breakfast yet. She still had time to exercise at least one horse. She'd keep a close watch and when she saw a light in the kitchen, she'd know the cook was up and going about her business. She'd slip in the back door, introduce herself, sneak up that little narrow servant's staircase to the bedroom wing, and clean up to meet her executioners.

By the light of the lantern she'd lit when she first came to the barn, and the promise of dawn from over that eastern mountain, she saddled up the horse in the last stall. Not knowing where they usually rode to exercise the animals, she gave him enough rein to let him prance down the lane from the road up to the house. When they reached the end of lane, she turned him to the left and rode him what she fig-ured was half a mile down the road. A big oak tree desper-ately hanging on to its leaves became her turn around point.

Riding felt good. The horse was obedient even if he was frisky. She'd forgotten the joy of hard work before daylight and the exhilaration of a good morning ride. Hoping that she had time to ride at least one more horse before the family arose, she took the horse back to the stable, unsaddled him, and was in the process of rubbing him down as she hummed a fast Mexican melody she'd heard many times at the dances in Texas. She checked the windows as she rode back down the lane and sure enough the kitchen window had a nice yel-low glow. The cook must be up and around, she thought, so she'd have to get the horse back in his stall quickly.

"Who are you and what are you doing?" a feminine voice asked from behind her.

Douglass jumped, startled at the sound. As she opened her mouth to explain who she was and what she was doing, she suddenly felt the barrel of a shotgun stick into her shoulder blades. She raised her arms slowly, showing the woman she wasn't carrying a weapon.

"Horse thief, are you? Turn around slowly and don't you try anything. You're probably one of those Rebel drifters trying to steal our best horse to get back to your worthless home," the woman said.

Douglass turned slowly. So she was to be shot for a Rebel drifter horse thief instead of a liar. Not that it mattered, dead was dead. She'd traveled all these miles, too stubborn to be rescued by her brothers at any time, only to find two shot-gun shells with her name engraved on them both. "Easy on that trigger finger," she said hoarsely to the lovely blond-haired woman holding the gun.

"Not on your life, drifter," the woman said. "I can tell by your accent you're a Rebel and I'm not taking chances. You were going to steal our horse and probably burn the barn as you left. You Rebels are good at burning and killing. Good thing I saw the light and brought the gun to see what was going on out here."

"I'm not burning or stealing anything," Douglass said.

"I guess not. Not with a gun in your face. Now you march toward that house right slowly. Aunt Laura will figure out what we're to do with you."

Douglass started to tip her wide brimmed hat to let her braids fall down her back. Maybe if the woman realized she was dealing with a female she wouldn't get an itchy finger from the stables to the house.

"Don't you touch that hat!" the woman said icily. "You probably got a gun or a knife hiding up there and I'm not taking any chances with a wild Rebel like you. Now march slow-like and remember I'm not one bit afraid to pull this trigger. It'd be a pleasure, as a matter of fact. I'd gladly see you die to help pay the debt for you mean Rebels setting fire to my house and killing my parents."

Douglass heard the raw pain, fear, and hatred in the woman's voice and marched slowly toward the house, praying all the time that her two brothers, Colum and Flannon, would come riding down the side of the mountain, a Rebel scream piercing the air, and rescue her before she was nothing more than a dead body, the Yankee soil soaking up her Rebel blood. Evidently God was part Irish and holding a grudge against her for her wicked lies, because her prayers were not answered.

Monroe stretched and wiggled down in his bed like a child. He was home at long last. The war was over; his last jobs were finished. Nothing could possibly go wrong from here on out. A vision of Douglass danced across his mind and he moaned. He'd forgotten about her for a few moments there. Oh well, he could have breakfast with his mother, sister, and cousin before Douglass even awoke. He'd tell them about her, but he would leave out some of the story. They didn't need to hear about the horse stealing or the lies. He

waited a minute before he crawled out of bed, trying to figure out the best way to tell them why he'd brought her all the
way home with him when at any time he could have sent her
back to Texas.

The commotion in the kitchen was music to his ears as he
took the narrow back stairs. He could hear Indigo's voice
floating up through the aroma of frying ham, and then his
mother telling her something about Ellie already going to
the barn to do part of the cleaning before breakfast. He stood
at the bottom of the enclosed staircase for a few minutes,
soaking up the happiness of a new morning in familiar sur-
roundings. Then he stepped out into the kitchen and waited
for them to see him.

Laura Hamilton's face went white when she noticed her
son standing there in the corner. "Oh my," she exclaimed
and ran across the room to wrap her arms around him in a
fierce hug. "You scared me, son," she said.

Indigo was right behind her with hugs for her oldest
brother and a silly smile pasted on her face. "When did you
get here?" She finally pulled away from him, leading him by
the hand to the stove where she flipped the slices of ham
over to brown the other side. "I'm afraid to let go of you
because you might be a dream," she said. "Why didn't you
wake us up when you came in?"

"It was very late." He yawned. "But I smelled breakfast
creeping up the stairs so I had to get up early and see what
was going on down here."

"Your friend, the one you brought home with you. The
one you mentioned in the telegram. Is your friend still sleeping?" Indigo asked.

"Of course. Douglass won't get up until noon. I caught the
devil because I wouldn't rent rooms in Shirleysburg and
come in today, but two miles is nothing in the dark when you
know the way. So, anyway, I put Douglass in one of the spare
rooms. Sometime today Gus at the livery stable is sending
someone out to get the buggy I rented to get us here. Is that

food about ready? I'm starving." He hugged his little sister close to his side.

"Got to scramble a skillet of eggs and slice the bread, then it's ready," she said.

"You've grown in the past year and a half. You're almost as tall as me," he said, finally letting go of her so she could finish cooking.

"Well, I would hope I'm finished growing," Indigo said. Her deep blue eyes sparkled. What did her brother think she'd done while he was gone? Shrunk?

"And why would that be?" Monroe asked.

"Because I'm taller than a lot of the men around here already. Nobody will want to marry a giant. Men like little women who simper and are delicate." She giggled, tossing her chestnut braid back over her shoulder.

"Not all men," he said, remembering Douglass and cutting off a sigh. She might be a small woman but there wasn't a simpering bone in her body, and delicate wasn't a word in her vocabulary either. Not even when she danced at the White House did she come off as a delicate little flower. Not Douglass Esmerelda Sullivan. She cut a wide swath wherever she went, and once they got over the shock of the story he was about to tell them, they'd love her as much as he did.

Love her? Great balls of red hot fire! He didn't love Douglass. Any man with a brain rattling around in his head wouldn't love that snappy, hateful, determined bag of Texas sass. Thank goodness her brothers would arrive soon to fetch her back to that flat land full of heat, mosquitoes, and egos— all enormous as elephants.

"You look like you ate a sour pickle. Whatever were you thinking about?" His mother patted his shoulder to make sure he was right there in the kitchen with her. She hadn't expected him for at least two more days. She and Indigo had been planning to make him his favorite apple pie on the day she figured he'd be riding down the lane. But a surprise was nice too. Laura tucked an errant strand of bright red hair, now streaked with silver, behind her ear. It was good to have her oldest child home, for sure. She and the girls had managed, and they'd been more fortunate than some, like Ellie's parents, who'd lost their home and lives in the Chambersburg fire. But it would be wonderful to have a man back in Love's Valley. When Henry Reuben and Harry Reed were back, then they could go back into full production and buy a few more horses.

"No, I just had a shocking revelation," Monroe admitted.

"What? That I've been looking at men?" Indigo teased, scooping the eggs into a crock bowl and setting them in the middle of the table.

"I suppose I better holler for Ellie to come on in and eat. She'll be so surprised to see you, but after her shock wears off I'm sure she'll coerce you into helping her in the stables." Laura's brown eyes twinkled.

"Gladly. Anything but riding on stagecoaches, in train cars, and sleeping wherever we could find a room," Monroe said, his mind still reeling from the feelings he'd just admitted having for Douglass. He'd have to do what she said—fall out of love. Besides, it wouldn't work anyway. She was not only a Rebel, she was half Mexican and half Irish. Laura Hamilton would pitch a fit seen only in the front gates of heaven when a priest was denied entrance through the pearly gates if he told her he was in love with Douglass. No, it would never work, so he'd never mention the idea. The nice thing about the revelation was that he'd discovered his heart wasn't a big ball of scar tissue that would never love again. When he fell out of love with that Southern baggage, maybe he would find someone else more suitable to be a companion to him for the rest of his life.

"So tell us more about your friend." Laura started toward the back door. "No, wait until I get Ellie and you'll only have to tell it one time."

"That's a good idea." He shook his head. *But I don't intend to tell you that I've fallen in love with her,* he thought. *That I want to hold her and kiss her every day the way I did when she nearly fell out of that boxcar. That I want to wake up with her in bed with me, without a chair between us. When did this happen? When? Now how am I going to face her when she comes down those stairs sometime later this morning, knowing that she's falling out of love with me while I'm falling in love with her?*

Laura was reaching for the door knob when suddenly the door swung open and a dirty little dark-skinned boy marched resolutely into the kitchen, Ellie right behind him with a gun only inches from his back.

"Look what I found trying to steal a horse out in our stables. A Rebel drifter who was most likely going to burn the barn as he left," she said. "I brought him to the house, Aunt Laura. You think we should ride into town with him? Sheriff Ryan would lock him up until the judge comes through."

Douglass looked across the room at Monroe sitting at the head of the kitchen table, a platter of ham in the middle of it, along with scrambled eggs and sliced bread. Their eyes locked somewhere in the middle of the room and a grin twitched at the corners of her mouth. She was starving nigh unto death, had done a full day's work before daylight, and she wasn't going to get a single chunk of that luscious-looking ham. Saved from shotgun shells to starve because no self-respecting Yankee was about to let a Rebel drifter thieving arsonist have a bite of breakfast before they turned the mean critter over to the sheriff.

"Herman Monroe, you can take care of this problem later. Lock him in the cellar for now," Laura said. "We'll have our breakfast and then—" She stopped mid sentence when she saw her son's face pale. He was staring right at the intruder as if he knew the boy, yet there was something else there. High color filled his dark, handsome, stubble-covered cheeks.

"Herman?" Douglass said in a high-pitched voice. "Herman? No wonder you didn't want anyone to know your name. Herman Monroe Hamilton. Herman?" she said again before she bent over and gave in to the worst case of giggles she'd ever had. It didn't matter if they were going to put her in a cellar with no food and cart her off to the sheriff's to hang for a crime she didn't commit. She had committed the same crime earlier and had gotten off scot free so maybe she was going to have to pay for that one after all. Not to even mention all the mean lies she'd told. She'd look out in the crowd gathering to watch her hang and giggle the whole way. If they asked her for last words, she'd say, "Herman Monroe," and giggle all the way to the pearly gates.

Herman! That would most certainly help her fall out of love with him. If there was an uglier name in the whole world, she didn't know it. When she thought of Herman she recollected the old wino derelict who lived in the room behind the saloon in DeKalb. He swept the floors of the bar everyday and drank up his pay every night. His teeth were stained chocolate brown with years of chewing tobacco and every child in DeKalb kept out of his way.

"Herman?" She got the hiccups and straightened up, her sombrero falling on the floor in front of her.

"Esmie!" Monroe said just as hatefully. Lord, what ever made him think even for a minute that she'd captured his heart. What an embarrassment to have her standing there acting like someone's kid sister who wasn't quite right in the head.

"Herman Monroe, what is going on?" Laura narrowed her eyes and stared at him.

"That's right, Monroe, and when did you get here anyway?" Ellie lowered the gun in bewilderment. It was plain as the sun coming up over the mountain these two knew each other. And good grief, that was a braid hanging down his back. Was this one of those Chinese boys and not a Rebel drifter at all? Ellie wondered.

The tableau hung in total silence for an eternity while Monroe and Douglass continued to stare at each other across the room, both blushing scarlet, Douglass trying to get her giggles under control.

"Are you going to tell us what's going on?" Laura asked curtly. "Well, my goodness, you aren't a boy at all. You're a girl," she said when she saw the braid and realized that the shape of the young person in her kitchen left no doubt that she was in fact a girl.

"Yes, ma'am, that I am," Douglass said. "And I wasn't stealing a horse. Not this time. I couldn't sleep so I cleaned the stables like I do at home in the early morning hours. If ya'll want to take a little trip out there and check, you'll see I'm telling the truth. The reason I had that horse out of the stall was because I had ridden him for exercise. I'll have to show you how to build a round exerciser so the horses can all have a run every day. Besides, Herman Monroe," she giggled again, "said you people get up before the crack of dawn to go to work and I didn't want anyone to think I was a sluggard. You're not going to like me anyway, and I wanted to be sure I did my part before my brothers arrived to rescue me."

The soft Southern drawl mesmerized them all. Indigo frowned like her mother. Ellie still looked like she'd like to shoot her, female or not. Monroe narrowed his eyes, daring her to go on any further.

"So, Herman Monroe, are you going to introduce me?" Douglass asked. "Sorry I didn't have time to wash the horse manure off my britches or my face." She took off her gloves and shoved them into her pocket, then pushed back a few strands of long, straight black hair.

"Introduce you?" Laura asked.

"Yes, Mother, introduce her," Monroe said. "You know I mentioned bringing a friend home with me for a few days. Well, I suppose we'd better tell you our story while we have breakfast. Set that gun over in the corner, Ellie. She wasn't stealing a horse, not this time. Not that she's above doing that, but if she'd wanted to steal a horse, you wouldn't have caught her that quickly. Douglass, the lady who brought you in is my cousin Elspeth who lives here with us now. The cook back there is my baby sister Indigo, and this is my mother, Laura Hamilton," he said pointing at each of them.

"And this is Douglass Esmerelda Sullivan." He nodded toward Douglass, who looked worse than she had since the time he'd seen her sitting in the middle of the road. And twice as beautiful.

"But I thought Douglass was a man," Laura whispered. "You said a friend, Douglass, in your telegram." She literally fell into a chair beside the table.

"No, ma'am, I'm all girl. The reason I've got a boy's name is Daddy is a pure Irishman and Momma is Mexican. They decided before my first brother, Patrick Cordona, was born that Daddy could name all the children their first name and Momma would name the middle one. After six boys, Daddy gave up thinking he'd get an Irish Colleen and had the name Douglass picked out for me. When I was a girl, the shock was so great he kept the name," Douglass said, hearing the South in her voice, but there wasn't a thing she could do about it. If they didn't like Rebels then so be it, she couldn't be anything other than what she was.

"Sit down, Douglass," Monroe said. "We'll tell them while we eat."

"Not on your life, Yankee," she declared. "Now that I don't have a gun in my back, I'm going up those stairs and changing out of these clothes and washing up. I'll not be sitting down to a meal looking like this."

"You might as well," Ellie said curtly. "If you're not a thief, and you're really going to stay, then I could use some help after breakfast with the horses, and you'd just have to change again. Besides, by the time you change the eggs will be cold and greasy. That's not saying I've changed my mind about you Rebels, though."

"Well, it'd take more time than you've got to make me change my mind about you Yankees, but I do enjoy working the horses, so if you'll excuse me a half a minute, I'll wash up in that water over there." She pointed toward the pump at the end of the dry sink. "Breakfast looks good Indigo, and Mrs. Hamilton. I suppose you two are the cooks?"

Indigo shot her a look meant to drop her in her tracks. A Rebel sitting up to her breakfast table, even if she was a friend of Herman Monroe's, almost curdled her stomach. Lord, there wouldn't be a dignified Yankee in the whole state who'd come calling if word got out. "I'm of the same mind as Ellie. When are you leaving?"

"Girls . . ." Laura cautioned half-heartedly, wondering the same thing.

"As soon as possible," Douglass threw over her shoulder as she washed her hands and face. "Not one minute past the time my brothers ride over that ridge and rescue me from this godforsaken place."

Chapter Thirteen

Laura ate a hearty breakfast while listening to Douglass and Monroe tell their story. Mostly, she kept an eye on her son, who couldn't take his eyes off that mysterious-looking woman. Though she was dressed in britches and a man's shirt, and her hair was nothing more than a long ropy braid down her back, she was a magnificent beauty. She had soft, lightly-tanned, unblemished skin and dark eyebrows shading the lightest, crystal clear blue eyes Laura had ever seen. That Herman Monroe had fallen in love with the woman during the past weeks was so evident that it produced a cold chill down Laura's backbone.

She'd move heaven and earth and buy half of the state of Texas to get her son the wife he wanted. After the statements he'd made before he was sent to Galveston, Texas, concerning never having a warm heart again after what all he'd seen, it was a delight to watch him interact with Douglass. What a name! She'd never get used to calling a woman by a name like that.

"So you're a liar as well as a Rebel?" Ellie asked bluntly.

"That I am," Douglass nodded. "And it's gotten me into more trouble than any one woman deserves, but I'll step up to the bar and face the music for my misdeeds. I'm sorry for all the trouble I've caused with my lies. And believe me I will pay for them the rest of my life. My family will see to it. How far is it to a Catholic church? I expect I'd better go

153

to confession. But then when my brothers come and haul me back to Texas, I expect I'll have lots of time to do that." She didn't mention that part of her penance would be loving a man and not being able to have him.

"You deserve whatever they make you do," Indigo declared.

Douglass was almighty glad Monroe hadn't told them about the times they'd had to share a bed or the time they'd been caught by the lady of the night in the brothel. These two tactless women would have really crawled up on their soap boxes if they'd known that.

"Yes, if the truth be known, I probably do deserve it." Douglass nodded honestly. "If I had it to do over again and know what I know now, I'd have seen through Raymond Pierce's deception. But a person can't go back and undo what's already done. I'm a survivor just like ya'll women are so I can just go forward with my chastised heart. If we weren't the survivors we are, we'd be causalities of this war that's made us both leery of the other. So I told lies and it was wrong. The only thing that it did was buy me some time for my brothers to ride off the edge of their mad. They'll still be fuming, with steam coming out their ears and fire from the top of their heads by the time they get here, but at least the bad edge will be gone."

"Maybe I'll shoot them both," Ellie said without even a hint of a smile.

"If you do, go for the tallest one first. That'd be Colum. He's got the fastest draw amongst them all so you'll only have one chance. If you're going to draw a bead, make sure you kill him dead or else say your prayers for forgiveness because he'll shoot first and ask questions later." Douglass finished off the last of her bread with a spoon full of wild plum jam.

"He wouldn't shoot a woman," Ellie said.

"Don't bet on it," Douglass replied. "Now you ready to go take care of exercising those horses or are we going to wash up these dishes first?"

"I'll do the dishes. This is *my* kitchen," Indigo said. No Rebel woman was going to taint her dishes.

"Yes, ma'am. Thank you for a fine breakfast. You are a very good cook. I'd be glad to take you home with me to Texas. Daddy would give you a job in the kitchen. He likes good fluffy scrambled eggs and ham," Douglass teased.

Indigo shot her the meanest look she could conjure up. "Tell her that I'm a Hamilton, Monroe. That I cook because I want to not because we can't afford to hire help. Tell her that I wouldn't go to Texas or any other of those wretched Southern states for all of the money in the world. Tell her those things because I don't intend to speak to her again."

"Indigo!" Monroe raised an eyebrow.

"That's alright. I was making a joke," Douglass said. "Guess you Northern women are so straight-laced and stiff-necked you don't even recognize a compliment. Stealing cooks in Texas is considered a hanging offense, but we all tease about it. When we go to someone's house for dinner, the highest compliment we can pay that household is to offer to take their cook home with us. Sorry I stepped on toes. And it's alright if you don't want to speak to me, Indigo. Can't say I'd want to speak to some Yankee who coerced Colum into bringing her home to save her hide, either."

"I think I'll go help exercise the horses," Monroe said. "I'd planned on taking a look at the land this morning and sniffing up lots of mountain air, so I can kill two birds with one stone."

"While you're throwing stones, try killing some Rebels," Indigo said, flouncing off to the other side of the big kitchen to fill a tea kettle to heat the dish water.

Douglass made her escape before the younger sister began throwing more than barbed words at her. At least her skin wasn't flayed, she hadn't been locked in a damp old root cellar, and her stomach was full. That all they'd done was fuss and mouth was a blessing—even if the words had stung.

"I suppose I should apologize for their behavior," Monroe

said, following her to the stables. "You did very well in there, though, I must admit."

"Well, I didn't have jack squat help from you. After you got finished telling them how it was I came to be with you on the trip home, you didn't say anything in my defense," she said. "Sure enough makes it a lot easier to fall out of love with you when you act like that. Want to kiss me right here in the middle of the yard in your precious Love's Valley to see if I'm making any progress?"

"I don't think so," he lied. His arms ached to draw her so close her heart would beat a little too fast in unison with his. He would give anything just to feel that surge carousing through his whole body.

"Afraid they'll see you from the kitchen window and grab that shotgun from behind the door?" she taunted.

"Nope, afraid I'll have as much trouble as you if we share anymore of those kisses."

She raised an eyebrow. "Well, ain't that the funniest thing ever. You've fallen in love with me, Herman Monroe Hamilton, and now you've got to fall out of love too. Let me tell you something, honey, it ain't an easy job. I'm not so sure a Yankee can even do it. It takes a lot of determination."

"You saying you're stronger than I am because you're a Rebel? Girl, we beat you in a war. Besides, you're just a little girl. How old are you anyway?" he asked. Standing out in the middle of the yard arguing like two little kids wasn't the way a man told a woman he'd fallen in love with her.

"What is this day? I kind of lost track with all the traveling. Seems like I ran away with that skunk Raymond around the first of September." Her brow furrowed trying to remember.

"This is Thursday, October fifteenth," he said. "What's that got to do with your age or falling out of love?"

"I'm twenty years old today. And honey, the war might've been different if they'd let me fight. I reckon I could have whipped half the Yankees with one hand tied behind my back and an eye patch over my right eye," she said. "How old are you?"

"Today is your birthday?" he asked incredulously.

"Is it yours too?" she asked right back.

"No, my birthday is in August. I'm twenty-eight," he said.

"Mercy me, an old man. Why, you'll be losing your hair and teeth before long. You'll be getting fat and forgetful," she threw back over her shoulder, leaving him standing there in awe.

"Well, you're still a little girl. Far too young for me. You're barely out of short skirts." He took long strides to catch up with her.

"Right, darlin', and don't you forget it." She laughed. "I'm riding the last horse down there. That big old buckskin. I'll go north and you can go south. Wouldn't do for such a mismatched pair to spend the morning riding together, now would it?"

He busied himself finding a bridle, blanket, and saddle for his favorite horse and let her have the last word. It was a small price to pay since he'd have the last laugh. That buckskin was the orneriest creature ever brought to Love's Valley. The only man who'd ever been able to sit that horse had been his father, and Harrison Milford Hamilton had been dead six years. When old Lucifer was exercised, whoever did the honors walked him up and down the lane a few times, leading him by the reins.

Monroe stroked his horse General down the white blaze on his face and whispered how much he'd missed him. He led him out to the yard and saddled him up, keeping a sharp eye on Douglass as she led Lucifer out of the stall. Even though she whispered in his ear and kissed him between the eyes, making Monroe turn a faint shade of green with jealousy, she need not think she could charm that old devil into submission like she had Stony back in Texas.

Monroe got the bit and bridle set absolutely right and then tossed a blanket over General's back. So she planned to

ride one way and expected him to ride the other, did she?
She was wrong. He was going to ride right along with her
so he could pick her up when Lucifer tossed her off his back
into the bushes. And he was going to laugh the whole time,
right out loud, enjoying the whole experience. He began to
make bets with himself as to how far she'd get even if she
did get the saddle on Lucifer's back. To the end of the lane
before she found herself hanging on for dear life? No, not
that far. Probably not even past the house. Matter of fact,
she might not even get two steps. Six years was a long time
for Lucifer not to endure a rider. He'd probably pitch a fit
from the time she threw the blanket over him.

Suddenly Monroe's heart pricked him sorely. He'd have
to watch her carefully to keep Lucifer from rearing up and
actually hurting her. A simple toss into the bushes might
make her sore and wound her pride, but if the horse reared
and came down on her with all that weight behind those
front hooves, he could kill the little wisp of nothing. She
wasn't a big woman to begin with, and in ratio to Lucifer she
surely wasn't bigger than a bar of lye soap after a hard day's
wash.

Douglass caught Monroe's glances and figured she
must've chosen a horse that wasn't very docile, so she
worked her magic on him. She whispered soft words the
whole time she put the bit and bridle on, then when he shied
at the blanket, she calmed him with a lump of sugar she'd
hidden away in her pocket from the breakfast table. He was
skittish the whole time she settled the saddle, tightening it
up and adjusting the stirrups to fit her short legs, so she
picked up the reins and walked him all the way around the
stables. By the time she got back, Monroe was sitting on his
horse, his strong arms thrown over the saddle horn, waiting.

It's swim or drown time, she thought, trying to relay her
feelings to the horse through the touch of her fingers. *You be
a good boy now and don't be throwing me. My pride has
already taken a beaten by the women in this valley. I don't*

need you to add to it. Just let me exercise you and I'll give you so many sugar lumps tomorrow you'll have rotten teeth.

She put a boot in the stirrup and hoisted herself gracefully astride the saddle. Bulging muscles and tension met the soft squeeze of her thighs. For a second short of eternity, she thought he was going to sling her halfway back to Texas rather than let her take control of him. Abulita would drop dead in a screaming heap if she'd seen her only daughter riding without a sidesaddle in the presence of an eligible bachelor, even if he was a Yankee. But Douglass was glad for the man's saddle because if the horse got any more nervous, she would have a better chance of hanging on that way.

Monroe waited for Lucifer to put his head down and begin bucking off the unwanted weight on his back. It didn't happen. The horse didn't look as happy as he did when Harrison took him out for a morning run, but it did appear he was going to take a few steps without pitching Douglass off first rattle out of the bucket. Monroe adjusted his bet. They might make it to the end of the lane after all.

"Ready?" he asked.

"As I'll ever be," she said. "This horse hasn't been ridden in a while, has he?"

"Quite a while." Monroe nodded.

They rode side by side to the end of the lane where she turned north. She'd ride to the oak tree, and hope she didn't have to walk back because she found herself lying flat on her back in the road when the horse bucked her off. One thing was for sure, the old boy would have to go home eventually because two mountain ranges fenced him in. When Monroe fell right in beside her, headed north, she frowned. This wasn't what she'd wanted at all. Falling out of love with the man wouldn't be easy with him beside her all the time. And now he'd about half admitted that he was in love with her too. Now wasn't that a total laugh. Monroe—a captain in the Union Army, who owned or at least partly-owned a whole valley, small as it was—even looking at a half Mex-half

Irish woman. He'd better at least use a little sense and not voice such a thing to his sister, cousin, or mother, or her brothers would never find her body when they did come swooping down the side of that mountain. If Indigo could cut her to pieces with that sharp tongue of hers when all she thought was that Monroe and Douglass were friends, then what would happen if Indigo found out they'd fallen in love?

Douglass shuddered at the thought.

"This is where we will plant wheat next spring," Monroe said. "This part of the Valley has lain fallow since we three men went off to war."

"So the women took care of the horses and the house?" Douglass asked, grudgingly giving them a little credit where it was due.

"Yes, they did. Did you see that long, low building on the south side of the house? That's the bunkhouse where our hired hands lived. We usually kept about twenty in addition to some help in the house. When war came they all went to fight, and the house help—two cleaning girls, a gardener, and a cook—left too. No one wanted to stay back in the valley when they could be in the city. The cleaning girls were married to two of the hired men, so they went home to their families until their men came back. The cook went to stay with her daughter-in-law when her son went to the war," Monroe explained. "Now that I'm home and Henry Reuben and Harry Reed will be coming in a few months, I'll hire more help come spring. We'll have the whole valley green by next year; wheat and corn, hay for the horses."

Douglass nodded. "And how are you going to afford all this hired help? Didn't you lose your fortunes in the war?"

"No, we did not," Monroe said. "Our fortunes are not in this valley. This is our home and we work the land we live on because we enjoy it. We weren't raised to be sluggards, but we don't really have to work at all. My father had investments in several companies that brought in our revenue. We like to see Love's Valley support itself."

Douglass had a dozen or more questions to ask, but it

didn't seem the right place or time. His money issues weren't really her business, not that it mattered one whit anyway, other than the fact that she wouldn't feel guilty eating whatever she wanted at his table. Or maybe she should say Indigo's table since the girl had let her know right quick that she wasn't to touch anything in that room.

"So what are we going to do about this thing between us?" Monroe asked out of the clear blue morning.

"Do? Why nothing," she said. "Why would we do anything? One time when I was a little girl there was this mean dog that wandered into our backyard. I was scared to death of that animal. It bared its teeth and growled every time I went out the backdoor. Finally I asked Daddy what I could do about that dog. You know what his answer was?"

Monroe shook his head, wondering why she was telling a story about a dog when he'd asked her a simple, straightforward question; one that had already begun to plague his heart even though he'd only just figured out he was in love with Douglass, who was twenty years old that very day.

"Well, you see, I kept thinking that if I fed that mean dog he'd take to me and quit being so ugly. So I'd been sneaking him bones and leftover biscuits. Daddy simply said if I wanted to remedy the matter to stop feeding that dog and he'd go away. For two days I didn't give him anything. By the third day he was gone. I figure it like this, Monroe: If I don't feed this love I have for you it'll be like that dog. It will go away. So no more of those kisses that knock my boots off and make me hear bells and music in the background. No more touching that sets my senses a-reeling, either. I won't feed the love and it will go away."

"I see . . ." Monroe replied, not believing a single word of it. If she left tomorrow, he'd still yearn for the jolt that surged through him when he held her.

"But you don't believe it, do you?" She raised a perfectly arched dark eyebrow at him.

"Can't say as I do, but we can give it our best try. Besides, you hate this godforsaken valley. You said so at breakfast.

And I hate Texas even worse. So love or no love, it won't work. Especially not with eight years between us."

"You got that right." *But it might have worked if you'd been willing to give it a try,* she thought. *The way my heart feels right now it could cozy right down with yours forever even if it had to live in this valley to do it. But we'll never know because you think I'm some little girl or puppy dog you saved from ruination and you'll never see me for the woman I am. Will I ever find another man who makes my heart feel like it does right now? And why, oh why, did I have to go and fall in love with the most unsuitable man on the whole face of the earth, anyway? Why didn't I just sit there on my trunk and not tell the lies that got me in this mess?*

Chapter Fourteen

Douglass inhaled deeply the clean, chilly air as she stepped off the back porch and started toward the stables. She held her skirts up to keep them from dragging in the dirt. She still cleaned the stalls and exercised the horses in her britches, which she had to wash every day after lunch, but in the afternoons she wore one of the two dresses Laura had given her. The hand-me-downs were two of Indigo's outgrown work dresses, and although she hadn't pitched an open fit about it, at least the girl had only given Douglass a sour look when she showed up wearing one the first day. Douglass couldn't help but think how much more sour the looks would have been if she'd come down those stairs wearing the dress she had worn to the White House social event.

Three days had passed since that first horrid morning. Laura was amiable enough in a standoffish kind of way. She was a lovely, dignified lady who Douglass would have liked to have known better, but the first thing she'd learned was that the Hamilton family was a fenced-in group of folks. The gate was locked and no one was allowed inside without permission, and no one had extended an invitation to her. Not even Monroe, who'd been careful to keep his distance since that first ride. They didn't tell funny stories about their childhoods at the supper table. They didn't pass out hugs in the middle of the day because they felt like it. Like the way in which she'd grown up, with grandparents and parents always ready to stop what they were doing to show affection toward her, she could tell there was love beneath the surface. Deep down in their souls the Hamiltons loved each other as much as the folks did in the South, they just didn't show it as openly. Douglass cocked her head off to one side as she strolled across the yard. It didn't make the Hamiltons or the Sullivans better parents. Not better, not worse, just different.

A prickly sensation set up an itch deep in her heart. Her brothers were getting close, she'd swear to it. The only time she felt like that was right before severe trouble came calling. Granted the feeling had failed her with Raymond Pierce, but most of the time it was as true as the sun rising in the East. Would it be today that they arrived? She hoped not. She wanted another day or two to think about this situation she'd gotten herself into with Monroe.

The doors to the stable were already open so Douglass slipped inside without making any noise. She fed Lucifer a couple of sugar lumps and told him how special he was. Ellie had been aghast that she'd ridden the horse that first morning, chastising her because no one had ever ridden him but her Uncle Harrison. From that point on, even though Ellie kept her distance, her words didn't freeze Douglass into a solid mass of ice like Indigo's tried to do.

"And all it took was riding you," Douglass whispered softly in Lucifer's ear. "I wonder what it'd take for me to get Indigo to respect me as a woman. Maybe I could get up and make breakfast. Show her that I can cook as well as ride. I don't think so. I'd rather take my chances with you, old mean devil, than have her come down those stairs and drop me in my tracks with one of those looks. She's going to be an old maid for sure if she don't learn better."

A soft chuckle hushed her mouth and made her turn quickly to see who'd been listening in on her one-sided conversation with Lucifer. She scanned the stables and found no one. Frowning she narrowed her eyes and made a more thorough search. Ellie and Laura were in the parlor discussing

Ellie's upcoming wedding the next spring when she slipped out the back door. Laura said it was time they put the war behind them and put on a big wedding for the whole area to attend. She and Ellie had their heads together talking about flowers and white satin. Indigo was in the kitchen peeling apples for a pie and had given her a "why-aren't-you-gone-I'd-like-to-see-you-dead" look. Monroe? At breakfast he'd mentioned working outside. What would he be doing in the stables?

Another laugh, this time louder, floated down the ladder attached to the side of the wall and leading up to the hay loft. What was so funny up there? she wondered. She was halfway up the ladder before the idea popped in her mind that perhaps she'd be interfering with a tête-à-tête. Monroe'd been distant toward her for three days and he'd said he was going to fall out of love with her. Could be one of those women from Shirleysburg had come to visit and they were in the loft. A green streak of pure jealousy shot through her veins and the vision of Monroe kissing another woman the way he'd kissed her was more than she could bear.

She poked her head up through the hole in the floor of the loft to find Monroe standing with his back to her. Shirtless. Her breath caught somewhere halfway down in her lungs and hung there. Muscles rippled across his broad back, glistening with sweat. He leaned on a pitchfork and laughed again.

She eased on up the ladder, stepping on the skirt tail at one point and almost falling backwards. "What is so funny?" she asked, slinging one leg into the loft, and showing a fair amount of petticoats and lace-edged drawers.

"Shhhh." Monroe brought his forefinger to his mouth. "Kittens."

"Where?" Her eyes widened.

He pointed. Sure enough there was four little kittens, barely old enough to waddle, tumbling all over each other at the end of the loft. She stood as still as he did, enjoying the sight.

After a few minutes they discovered they were being watched and scrambled back across the hay to the back of the loft.

"I love baby kittens." Douglass sighed.

Monroe picked up his shirt and slipped his arms into it. He'd worked up a sweat pitching hay down into the wagon at the bottom of the loft window, but now that he'd finished, the cool mountain air chilled him. "Did you need something?" he asked, his tone suggesting that she was interfering with his business.

"No, I was petting Lucifer and I heard you laugh."

"When do you think your brothers will arrive?" he asked, putting an end to the good times and reminding her that she was only there for a little while. He'd been careful to stay away from her as much as possible. Last night his mother asked him if they'd had an argument. He'd told Laura that they hadn't, but he didn't confide in her that he was passionately in love with Douglass. No, he'd never say those words out loud. There was no need in courting an idea so far-fetched. Douglass would be miserable in Pennsylvania. She'd never endure the cold winters or the mountains, and she'd already made it plain anyway: "God forsaken place. Falling out of love. Don't feed it and it will disappear."

"Ready to see me gone, are you? Well, not any more so than I'm ready to leave," she said, amazed at how slick the lie escaped her lips. Yes, indeed, she needed to go to confessional because she was still telling lies.

Clouds shifted over the afternoon sun and soft rain began to fall. The smell of it combined with the fresh mountain air sent her to the window to hold her hand out to catch the drops. She'd miss the cool air when she went back to Texas. There was something about the mountains, even if she didn't like being cooped up between them, that had oozed down into her heart these past days. She loved the fresh smell and the soft rain. Texas didn't get rain like that very often. The rain there was mostly fast and furious, much like the way the people lived.

"Be careful, you could fall." He finished buttoning his shirt.

"I'm not asleep. I won't roll out the window like I did the boxcar," she said, reaching out even farther to let the rain fall into her open palm.

Monroe tucked his shirt into his pants and pulled his suspenders up over his shoulders. She was beautiful in his sister's old dress and with all that black hair piled up on the top of her head in a twist. He longed to have the right to take out all the pins and tangle it up between his fingers. Sighing for what could not be, he took a couple of steps closer to the window to smell the rain. In a few weeks the rainy days would turn into snowy days. The nip of winter was already in the air in the mornings. He'd had to break a skim of ice from the watering trough hours earlier. There would be warm afternoons for a few more weeks, but the nights would warrant an extra blanket or two before the week was out.

Douglass inhaled the aroma of sweet rain mixed with a sweaty man and liked it so much she blushed. Lord Almighty, falling out of love was surely more difficult than falling in love. Monroe was close enough that she could have leaned slightly and touched him, but that would undo in a moment all the progress they'd both made these past three days. *Please, just one more of those tantalizing kisses,* her heart begged. *Just one more to keep me all the days of my life. I won't lie anymore if I can just have one.*

The answer was no.

Colum lay very still, hidden in the edge of the trees at the foot of the mountain. He and Flannon had been watching the house since daybreak. They'd slipped down the lane while the moon still hung low on the horizon and the sun had only barely begun to rise. They'd seen their sister, wearing britches and her hair braided down her back, make several trips to the manure pile at the back of the stables. So the Yankees had her working for them, did they? Making her muck out horse stalls. That was good enough for her, but it riled Colum that she should be working so hard for Yankees. If it was of her own free will in Texas, that was one thing. Someday she'd inherit her share of the horse ranch there, so it was only right she learn how to help run it. But to see her leaning against the door frame to catch her breath almost softened his heart.

But not quite.

He was still angry enough at her for leading him and Flannon on a wild goose chase halfway across the world to string her up by her toes and make her beg for mercy. That stunt in Arkansas when she bought a ticket to Conway would stick in his craw for a long, long time. That's what put them two days behind. If it hadn't been for that trick, they'd have caught her in Memphis, he was sure.

"Don't look to me like she's being held at gun point. You reckon she's married that Yankee?" Flannon asked.

"Not even Esmie is that fool hardy," Colum all but growled. He'd rather be pinching the white tops off chicken manure in the Texas heat than lying there in surveillance. But watch he would, until he caught her in a position where he could snatch her away from those Yanks and carry her back home to face the music. He'd sent telegrams home regularly so they'd be expecting them in the next few weeks. He hoped his mother and grandmother had picked out a suitable convent to put her in. That's what happened when a young lady was allowed to make her own decisions. He'd told his parents and grandmother for years that Esmie had too much freedom. Now look where it had gotten them. She'd run off with one Yankee, slept with another, and disgraced both the Sullivan and Montoya names.

Colum and Flannon ate cold biscuits at noon and planned one strategy after another. Should they go ahead and shoot the man who'd stolen their sister when he appeared at the stables? Colum had a fine view of him in the loft window but there was a breeze and he hated to take a chance of merely wounding the sorry sucker.

"There she is," Flannon whispered when Esmie went into

the stables. "Now's our time. She's in there with him and we can take him standing on our heads and cross-eyed. I haven't seen one other man all day, Colum. Let's go get her and get out of here before that stagecoach leaves that little town we come through."

"Just a minute." Colum pointed toward the window.

They watched silently as the man talked to their sister. Did he have no decency, carrying on a conversation half-naked in front of a lady? But he wouldn't view Esmie as a lady after sleeping with her in a brothel, would he? Then Esmie was in the window, holding out her hand to catch the soft rain. They couldn't hear any of the words being said but the language of the body left no doubt the man and their sister were more than just friends.

"Douglass," Monroe said hoarsely.

"Yes, Herman," she teased.

"Don't call me that."

She'd been looking straight into his deep brown eyes, trying to memorize every detail about them. If she never found a man who could make her heart race like Monroe Hamilton, then she'd not ever marry. It wasn't as if she'd have much of a choice anyway, not in Texas anyway. By now, the story would be all over the state, that she'd eloped with one man and threw him over for another—neither of which would marry her. The first because he figured she was beneath him; the second because he thought she was too young and had too much Rebel blood in her veins. Life sure wasn't fair, but she'd created the mess she was in, and she'd be woman enough to life with the consequences.

Something moved in the trees and she caught it in her peripheral vision. Then a mouse darted across her foot, making her jump. She lost her balance trying to kick the mouse and see what was moving at the foot of the mountain at the same time. With arms fluttering like butterfly wings, she grabbed at anything to keep from falling, finally lasso-ing Monroe around the neck.

He tried to maintain balance but it was in vain. Both of them tumbled out the window and into the soft, damp hay in the back of the wagon. One minute she was thinking about kissing him, the next he was stretched out on top of her in a hay wagon. She opened her eyes, caught her breath, tightened her hold on his neck, and pulled his mouth down to hers for a kiss that threatened to stop the rain. Every nerve from the top of her head to the soles of her feet tingled. She ran her tongue over his lower lip and shivered at the delightful way he moaned. Out of sight, out of mind would not work. She was still in love with him.

Ellie and Indigo had stepped out on the back porch to smell the rain just minutes before Monroe and Douglass fell. Indigo groaned when she saw the kiss. She was going to have to shoot that sorry Rebel yet. Ellie smiled. So that's the way it was. That's why Monroe had been so cranky the past three days when he should have been happy to be home. He'd fallen in love with Douglass. Now wasn't that a pickle; a sour one at that.

Indigo gasped and pointed. Two men were running from the tree line straight toward the hay wagon. They were both carrying long rifles and looked pretty serious. "Rebels!" she shouted and grabbed Ellie's hand, both of them speeding across the back yard to warn Monroe. What a way for him to die after having survived the war. Bewitched by a Rebel woman and then shot while kissing her.

Colum and Flannon were so intent on reaching Esmie to make sure she hadn't been killed in the fall that they didn't even see the women holding up their skirt tails and racing across the backyard. Colum reached the wagon first, grabbed Monroe by the shirt collar, and jerked him away from Esmie.

"You dirty Yankee, why'd you push my sister out of the window. I ought to kill you!" he yelled, drawing back his fist with the full intention of breaking the man's nose and blacking both his eyes with one hit.

Before he could slam his knuckles into Monroe's surprised face, there was a woman on his back, pulling his hair,
clawing his cheek and screaming in his ear something about
how he wasn't going to kill anyone. He tried to shake her
off but she hung on harder, jerking at his hair until there
was a bald spot. Blood flowed down his cheek from the
scratch she'd made with her fingernails and his hearing was
going to be damaged forever the way the banshee was
screaming.

Douglass sat up with a start. She'd been enjoying the most
passionate kiss yet and suddenly Monroe had flown back-
wards off her and all hell had broken loose. Colum had
appeared out of the gray sky and was threatening to kill
Monroe. Ellie came to his rescue by literally climbing
Colum's frame. Flannon tried to pull her off when he realized
Colum was bleeding and then Indigo hauled off and hit
Flannon with her fist and bloodied his nose.

The noise brought Laura onto the scene. She hurried
across the yard, took one look at Douglass' puffed, thoroughly kissed lips, and figured out the situation immediate-
ly. The first thing she did was pick up Colum's rifle where
he'd dropped it when that she-cat from hell's furnace
attacked him, and fired it into the air.

"That is enough!" she declared.

"He threatened to kill Monroe." Ellie pointed to the man
holding a bloody cheek.

"Well, he tried to kill Esmie," Colum pointed at Monroe.
"He threw her out the window and she drug him with her."

"All I did was hit that fool for trying to hurt Ellie," Indigo
said indignantly, holding her aching fist.

"I was trying to get her off his back. Look at what she did
to his face," Flannon said.

"And what have you got to say?" Colum eyed his sister
coldly.

"Not one blasted thing. You've said enough," she raised
up on one elbow. "I suppose you've come to take me home?

And I guess you haven't ridden off your mad either since I don't even get a hug."

"You don't deserve a hug, not after the stories we've been told. Besides, I'm bleeding and you need to cover up your petticoats and drawers. How could you, Esmie?" he asked.

"Oh, the bunch of you stop it," Laura said. "You must be Douglass' brothers. Come on in the house and we'll get you cleaned up and fed before you take her back to Texas. It's too late to start out tonight anyway, and its raining, so you can spend the night."

"Mother!" Indigo said, wide-eyed.

"Aunt Laura," Ellie echoed her.

"Don't either of you say one word. This is my ranch and I'll do what I want. These brothers saw things happening different than you did. You want to introduce us, Douglass?" Laura asked.

"The one with the blood on his cheek is Colum. The one holding his nose is Flannon. Ellie, you and Indigo are to be commended. I don't think there's ever been a woman whipped them before," Douglass said, picking wet hay from her hair. "Brothers, this is Monroe Hamilton, who's been a perfect gentleman in spite of the impressions you've gotten from your journey. This is his mother Laura, a very gracious hostess as you can well see. The blond-haired lady is Elspeth. We call her Ellie and she's a cousin. The dark-haired one is Indigo and she's Monroe's sister."

"Right glad to make your acquaintance," Colum said through gritted teeth. "Now, Esmie, you better start talking girl and keep the words coming or else you're headed for a long life of mediation and prayers. Did you marry this Yank?"

"Don't you threaten her." Ellie pushed her forefinger in his chest. "You don't have any right to judge her. You have jumped to conclusions. What makes you think you've got the right to judge what happened on their journey. And besides, if you weren't such a bully, she would have come home to begin with and not traveled all those miles in the company of a stranger. What kind of mean brothers are you that she'd go halfway across a continent rather than face your wrath? And no, they are not married."

"Me, a bully? I'm the one bleeding," Colum said.

"And I said that's enough fighting like a bunch of *children*," Laura exclaimed emphasizing that last word. "Follow me. Good lord, we're all standing here like we don't have enough sense to get in out of the rain."

She marched off toward the house. They followed. Ellie and Indigo right behind her. Colum and Flannon behind them. Monroe and Douglass bringing up the rear. Their hands brushed and he entwined his fingers with hers ever so tenderly and briefly, letting go when they stepped inside the kitchen, all seven of them a dripping mess. The tingle was there even with Colum and Flannon only inches ahead of her. She'd never know if she'd had more time if she might have convinced Monroe to stay in love with her.

The gig was up.

Chapter Fifteen

Douglass slipped out of Indigo's outgrown dress and hung it in the wardrobe. The other was draped over the back of a rocking chair in the corner of the room, still drying from the rain that morning. She fingered the dress she'd worn to the White House and the lovely blue one she'd worn in North Little Rock, along with the traveling suit, which was what she'd wear tomorrow morning. She'd don it the next morning, slide into the seat of the carriage Laura had offered, and wave goodbye to Love's Valley and to everyone in it.

She shut the wardrobe door and blinked back the tears. She wouldn't cry. No, she would not. She'd had the most wonderful adventure and just one of Monroe's kisses would be worth a whole lifetime behind the stone walls of a convent. She crawled into the middle of the bed and sat crosslegged, reliving each of the memories. Seeing him in all his handsome glory like a knight in shining armor, sitting on that big, black horse looking down at her. Stealing that same horse. The two evil men who kidnapped her, and how wonderful he felt when she threw herself into his arms. The subterfuge in North Little Rock when she and Geraldine told all those lies, and Monroe's innocence—even if he was a Yankee officer—in believing them. The worried look on his face when she'd been visiting with Varley in Memphis. Saving her when she fell out the boxcar door. The lazy steamship ride up the river to Washington, D.C. All of it melted together into a big ache right inside her chest. Tomorrow she'd be gone, never to see him again.

Douglass opened the doors out to the widow's walk, the cold night wind sweeping down from the mountains and making her shiver. She drew her robe more tightly around her shoulders. At least Colum and Flannon had both hugged her before she came up to bed. They'd even laughed at the way she'd sent them on a wild goose chase to Conway, Arkansas when the Hamiltons and Sullivans shared supper. They couldn't stay mad at her forever, so perhaps her parents would forgive her as well. She was truly, truly sorry for her mistake in judgement.

Thinking of her brothers, she figured miracles really did happen, so maybe she'd find forgiveness in the rest of her family. After all, there had sat two of her staunch South-supporting brothers at a Yankee table, eating their fried chicken and biscuits and conversing like they hadn't been eager to kill Yankees just months before. Colum would have a scar on his handsome face from a long scratch put there by Ellie, and Flannon's nose might be a bit crooked for the rest of his life, but Douglass had thought that neither one had ever been more handsome. Indigo's cobalt-blue eyes spit fire most of the evening. It was plain that she and Flannon would have never been friends even if they'd lived next door to each other, but Ellie was a little more mature and accepting even if it was evident that she physically hated Colum.

Light poured from the window of the room next to hers. She knew that would be Monroe's room because she'd paid close attention that first night to which room he went into when he'd settled her in the room she used. What would he do if she tapped gently on the glass double doors and asked if she could come inside his bedroom? What would he do if she asked if she might sleep with him tonight? She'd never know because she wouldn't do such a thing, not in Laura's house. It would be disrespectful to her, and to her brothers, who were finally believing the real story about all that had happened. She'd had a few moments with them before retiring when she explained the situation in the brothel. She didn't go into detail about the other times she shared Monroe's bed, or tell them that she was desperately in love with him.

"Goodnight, Monroe," she whispered, the sound carried away on the wind.

She carefully pulled the window shut, blew out the candle, and slipped beneath the sheets. She gave way to the pain in her soul and let the tears flow down her cheeks, wetting the pillowcase to saturation. Weeping for what could not be and wishing for the impossible, she grew up more in that night than she'd done in a whole lifetime of pampered existence in Texas.

Monroe paced the floor in his bare feet, not caring that the floor was ice cold. The nightmare was over and tomorrow she would be gone. Colum and Flannon had said they'd leave right after breakfast. They weren't bad men and, given different circumstances, Monroe could have liked both of them. It was hard to fathom that a year ago he would have been on the other side of the fence from them, willing to order both of them shot just for being Southern Rebels.

He fell back on the bed, his head bouncing off the pillow. The ceiling became a picture frame for a whole series of likenesses of Douglass. First was her sitting there like some kind of majestic queen on that trunk in the middle of the road. Then the night she tamed that big black horse that he'd ridden all through the war and he had awakened to find her gone with his horse and been forced to rescue her from those highway pirates. One of them had referred to her as Her Irish Majesty. Well, that man was a pure prophet. That's exactly what Douglass Esmerelda Sullivan was. An Irish queen with enough Mexican blood to give her even more fire.

The man who married her would have a nightmare of a

life, Monroe thought. There'd never be a peaceful moment, but . . . oh, the wild ride of it all. It would be like going through life on the back of a bucking bronc. Instead of reaching the end of his life with a sigh, he'd come flying around the corner to the Pearly Gates, memories making his old eyes glitter and screaming at the top of his lungs, "Whew wee, what a ride!"

The corners of Monroe's mouth turned up slightly at that vision. He laced his hands behind his head. They might have given it a whirl, the two of them, if the timing had been better. But the war was still a gaping wound in everyone's heart. Yankees didn't marry Rebels.

Not now.

Twenty years ago it might have been possible. Fifty years from then it might be possible. But not in 1866, one year after the war was over. It would take pure magic and a downright miracle to boot. He'd come home safe from battle after battle. He'd survived the disease, the hunger, the cold, the heat. All of it. He'd vowed if he ever made it home to Love's Valley again, he'd never leave. Monroe didn't break his vows. He wasn't going to Texas even if he did love a Texan.

"Goodbye Douglass," he whispered around a lump the size of a cantaloupe stuck in his throat. He shut his eyes and let the dreams come. He hoped to see her in his dreams every day for the rest of his life.

Douglass' eyes were a bit swollen the next morning. Monroe's were more than a little bit dull. He sat at one end of the breakfast table; his mother at the other. Breakfast had never tasted so bland to either of them. Colum and Flannon flanked her like two bookends. Ellie and Indigo sat on the other side of the long table. Talk was sparse and tension thick.

"Thank you ma'am for your hospitality," Flannon said when the meal ended. "Miss Indigo, I might kidnap you and take you home with us to show our cook how to make eggs that fluffy. You ever want a job cooking, you hightail it on down to DeKalb, Texas and tell my Daddy I said to hire you."

Indigo rolled her eyes and Monroe chuckled.

"Did I say something wrong?" Flannon asked, frowning at his sister.

"Just everything. You don't offer to steal cooks in the North," Douglass told him. "There's no need in prolonging this goodbye thing, now is there? I wasn't supposed to have ever been here, so I'll say thank you for putting up with me. Indigo, you are a wonderful cook. Ellie, thank you for not shooting me first and asking questions later that first morning. Goodbye Laura. And Monroe, thank you hardly seems enough for all you've endured. But it's all I've got to offer. Now let's go. You all stay right here and don't come to the porch to wave us goodbye. Even though you don't like me, I've become very fond of all of you. Even you and your mean looks, Indigo. Somewhere down in all that dislike is a woman not totally unlike me. One that I could have been friends with if things had been different. Anyway I hate goodbyes. I always cry. Don't look at me like that, Monroe. Of course, I cry. I'm a woman, after all. It took me weeks to stop carrying on when each of my brothers went off to war. Now I'm going out the door and I'm not looking back . . . except in memories. I'll cherish those for the rest of my life."

She pushed her chair back, swallowed hard, and kept her eyes away from Monroe. If he said one word, she'd melt in a puddle of humiliation and tears at the toes of his boots, begging him to love her as much as she did him. She kept her back straight enough to keep all the pieces of her broken heart from falling out on the shiny foyer floor as she walked outside and put herself into the carriage. Flannon had already tied the two horses to the back of the buggy. When they got to Shirleysburg, they'd catch the stage to somewhere around Frederick, where they'd ride the steamship as far as they could. Backwards. She was repeating it all back-wards and somehow it didn't mean a thing because she'd only be half a woman from then on. How could she be whole when her heart had been captured in a remote little valley between two mountain ranges?

She sat stoically waiting for her brothers to come take her to her punishment. It didn't matter anymore. If they didn't put her in a convent, then she'd put herself there. She deserved it. Without Monroe, nothing mattered anyway. And every day she'd pray that Monroe was kept safe in Love's Valley.

Alone.

Safe. Alone, she told herself, battling the tears. Never did she want him to kiss another woman. If he did, she'd come back and haunt him, she swore silently. She loved him enough to give him up, but there was enough hot blood flow-ing in her veins that she sure wouldn't want him to love any-one else.

Flannon pushed back his chair. He didn't have a speech to deliver so he figured he'd follow his sister out, drive the car-riage to town, and then put up with the sass all the way back to Texas. Lord, he'd rather fight a rattlesnake bare-handed and bare-footed than listen to her all that way. It didn't take a genius to see that she was in love with Monroe Hamilton, but any fool would realize that wouldn't work. Not a Yankee and a purebred, opinionated Southern Rebel. She'd have the North in an uproar within six months.

Colum followed suit. If Monroe had nothing to say then it was time to leave. The man looked like he'd fought the whole war single-handed. Come to think of it, he'd been through worse, traveling with Esmie for the past few weeks. He should be standing in the middle of the table dancing a jig instead of sitting there with a love-sick expression on his face. A love-sick expression? The idiot had fallen in love with Esmie. Well, he'd best get her on out of here in a hurry if that was the case. Such a union would never work.

It would be the worst thing in the whole world. Well, not the absolute worst. The worst would be if that English-looking woman, Ellie, ever looked at him with moon eyes. Heaven help the man who got tangled up with her. He'd understood by the conversation last night that she was already engaged. He hoped the man was the King of England because Elspeth already acted like she was a queen. *Her English Royalty* would be engraved on the honeymoon buggy and all the people would have to bow down in worship to the blond-haired witch who'd married the poor unsuspecting groom.

Flannon took his seat on the driver's side and Colum hopped up beside his sister. The three of them wore serious expressions as Flannon slapped the horse on the flanks with the reins. Finally, the whole ordeal was over. Now it was merely a matter of getting home.

"Wait!" Monroe yelled from the porch. "Just a moment, Flannon, please."

Douglass shut her eyes. She'd probably forgotten a handkerchief. Only honest Monroe would come running to bring it back. Then he was beside the carriage and her hand was in his, a jolt of electricity gluing her tongue to the roof of her mouth. A fleeting thought went through her mind that she must never let a man know he could affect her like that or else he'd have all kinds of power over her.

"Did you get the job done?" He was looking deeply into her face when she opened her eyes, his face so close it was practically out of focus.

"What job?" Flannon asked.

"Did you?" she returned, ignoring everyone and everything around her. The only thing that mattered as the sun stood still and time refused to move, was that Monroe was holding her hand.

"What are you talking about?" Colum asked.

"Both of you hush," she demanded. "Now, tell me, did you fall off that fence, Monroe? Did you fall in or out?"

"I fell in just like you did, and I've tried to get back on the fence and fall to the other side, but every time I do, my heart is so heavy it won't let me climb up there," he said.

"How poetic." She smiled.

"What about this 'godforsaken' place?" he asked.

"My heart sees things a bit differently now."

"It's cold in the winter."

"I reckon I could be warmed up if we didn't have a chair between us," she said.

"You got something to say to me then," he asked, a twinkle in his eye.

"I reckon the man is supposed to do that, but I'm not adverse to asking if you're a chicken-livered Yankee," she said with a chuckle.

"I love you, Douglass Esmerelda Sullivan. Will you marry me?" he asked, leaning forward to kiss her.

Magic.

Music.

Miracles.

"Yes," she whispered when the kiss ended.

"Well, halle-blasted-lujah!" Flannon threw his hat into the air. "Now I don't have to ride all the way to Texas with her."

Indigo stomped her foot so loudly that the glass panes in the front door rattled. "Now I have to put up with her every day forever. I'll marry the first blue-blooded Yankee who asks me to get away from here. Not that anyone is going to ask me if he has to accept a Southern-talking Rebel Texan as part of the family."

"Would you fellers stay on a week for the wedding?" Monroe asked Colum and Flannon. "We'll plan a simple affair and then you can go home."

Colum bit his tongue and nodded stiffly. He'd insist on living in the bunkhouse away from that Ellie woman. But like Flannon, he was grateful he wouldn't have to visit his spitfire sister in a convent. She'd have turned the whole religion around in the sight of a year.

"Good, that's a plan then. A week and I'll be your wife." Douglass slipped her arms around Monroe's neck and pulled his face down to hers.

"I love you," Douglass whispered in Monroe's ear, then kissed him one more time, enjoying the warm, mushy feeling down deep in her stomach.

Chapter Sixteen

Douglass pinned her hair back into a chaste bun and set the *peineta* just so at the top of the chignon. The lace *mantilla* fell over it perfectly that day. Instead of a new dress, she'd opted to wear the same one she'd worn when she danced at the White House. Somewhere Laura had begged a bouquet of the last of the fall roses from a neighbor who had a bush on the sheltered side of the house. The fragrant red blossoms were tied with a white satin ribbon.

"Is the bride ready?" Colum poked his head inside the bedroom door without knocking.

"Yes, she is," Douglass said. "Is it time?"

"Ten more minutes," he said. "Are you sure about this Douglass? You're not marrying him to keep from facing the music in Texas?"

"I'm sure," she said, telling the absolute truth. "I love Texas, Colum, and I'll miss it and my family so much I'll cry at times. But I love Monroe enough to live anywhere with him. I thought I loved Raymond, but I was mistaken. This is real and lasting, like Abulita has with grandfather and like Momma and Daddy have. My hope would be that all six of you Sullivan men find the same for yourselves."

"Well, honey, I might find it someday but it will sure enough be in Texas where the land and sky meet and not in this godforsaken place," Colum said seriously. "That wicked Ellie will start playing the piano soon. My face is never going to be the same." He touched the scab on his cheek.

"Makes you even more handsome," Douglass told him. "Send Indigo in, please."

"You don't know what you're getting into," Colum said. "The convent would be a picnic compared to living in this hole in the mountains with a bunch of Yankees. Monroe ain't too bad and his mother is a jewel. But Esmie, those two women are vicious. Ellie is downright cold and Indigo hates you."

"Just send her in." Douglass grinned.

She waited, listening intently for Indigo's footsteps on the steps, but another sound caught her attention. She heard soft weeping coming from the balcony outside. She cracked the door open and peeped out. Ellie leaned against a wall, her hands covering her eyes and her shoulders heaving.

"Ellie, what's the matter?" Douglass tossed her roses in the rocking chair and gathered the woman into her arms.

"It's your wedding. I won't spoil it," Ellie said.

"Do you not want me to marry him that badly? I promise I'll do everything to make him happy. I don't deserve him after the shameless things I did—lying to him, stealing his horse. But I'll do my best to be a good wife and I promise I won't ever lie to him again. He says he trusts me now," Douglass said soothingly.

"No, it's not that. I knew Monroe was in love with you from the beginning. It was all over his face and yours. It's my own fiancé. I was in a place I shouldn't have been earlier today. He was with a friend in the garden. I overheard what he said. I can't marry him and I can't not! I'm already past twenty and the wedding has been announced. It would be an embarrassment to the family for me to break it off now. Gossip would go rampant. He doesn't love me, Douglass. He's only marrying me to get his hands on the money my parents had. There is quite a lot of it and he wants it. He told the man to be patient and they'd have their hands on lots of money before the summer's end," Ellie said in between broken sobs.

"The sorry two-bit gutter rat!" Douglass said. "Get me a pistol. We'll shoot him and bury him under the compost pile with the rest of the horse manure."

Giggles replaced sobs as Ellie wiped away the tears. "I suppose if you can marry a Yankee, I can not marry one. I'll tell him before the night is out. You know, I think you and I might be friends after all."

"We can shoot him, honey. God wouldn't even lay the charge to our account. He might even overlook all my lies if I took care of a varmint like that," Douglass declared.

"He's not worth the bullet," Ellie said. "Now let's go have a wedding."

"Where are you?" Indigo stepped out onto the balcony. "Well, rats. I thought maybe you'd changed your mind and committed suicide by jumping over the railing to your death on the stones below."

"Not hardly," Douglass said. "I'm marrying your brother and we're building a house up the valley. Next year I'll be out of your hair, darlin', but for that year you and I are going to have to live in pretty close quarters. You don't have to like me, Indigo. But we both love Monroe. You love him as a brother. I love him as a man. And neither of us is going to hurt him, are we?"

Indigo shot her one of those famous looks but it bounced off Douglass like hail off a tin roof. "Is that a threat, you misplaced Southerner?"

"I don't make threats, darlin', I state facts. Now Ellie is going down to start the music. You are my bridesmaid, since I don't have a sister until after Monroe and I take our vows. Then, like it or not, you and I are sisters. We can make the best of it or the worst. I'm willing to go for the best, but honey, if you want the worst, I can provide it. I grew up with six Irish-Mexican brothers. You only had three soft-hearted old Yankees, so my training is a bit better than yours." Douglass picked up her bouquet and smiled sweetly to her soon-to-be sister.

Indigo grinned and followed Ellie down the stairs. She might decide to like Douglass after all, but it would be a long, long time before she ever let her in on the secret.

The ceremony lasted an hour. To Monroe and Douglass there were no other people in the room and it lasted forever. When the priest finally gave them permission to seal their vows with a kiss, Douglass tossed her bouquet to Ellie and wrapped her arms around her husband's neck, pulling his mouth down to hers.

"I'm in love with you," she whispered. "Really, really in love with you."

"And I'm in love with you, heaven help me," he whispered back.

"Honey there ain't enough power even up there to help you now. You've got me for all eternity," she said. "We're in Love's Valley where miracles and magic happen."

"Amen." He grinned and the two of them turned around to face their families.